Postcard from Nice

A Novella

Kyle Hunter

Copyright 2024 by Kyle Hunter. All rights reserved.
Published in the United States by Monceau Publishing.
P. O. Box 40152
Raleigh, NC 27629
www.Kyle-Hunter.com

No portion of this publication may be copied, retransmitted, reposted, duplicated, or otherwise used without the express written approval of the author. Any unauthorized use of any part of this material without permission by the author is prohibited and against the law. The only exception is brief quotations in printed reviews.
This is a work of fiction. Names, characters, and situations are products of the author's imagination and are used fictitiously. Any resemblance to persons living or dead is entirely coincidental.

Cover design by Erika Alyana Sañga Duran.

ISBN 979-8-9895265-5-0

More novels by Kyle Hunter

Circle Back Around
One December
Postcard from Nice *(A Novella)*

Provence Series

Prodigals in Provence
A Promise in Provence

The Second Chance Series

Marissa Rewritten *(A Novella)*
Julia Redesigned
Sydney Rewound
Eden Redefined

The Brenner Falls Series

Good Gifts
Custom Made
Embracing the Broken

Postcard from Nice   *Kyle Hunter*

Chapter One

Meghan Clark shuffled papers across her desk as she scanned the space for her phone. Normally, she wouldn't have her personal phone anywhere near her on a workday. Especially *this* workday. Like neck-high frothing waves, two high-priority projects threatened to drown her. But she was on the threshold of wrapping them up. Once they were done, she'd be able to breathe again.

She cut another glance at her phone. A compulsion. An unhealthy addiction. But Adam said he'd call when he got back to town. He hadn't, though he should have arrived in the early afternoon. Normally, she wouldn't be this anxious, but things had been off between them for a month or so. He'd insisted things were fine. Which itself *wasn't* fine.

"Meghan, is everything ready for the Simmons-Burnett engagement dinner tonight?"

She lifted her gaze to her boss, Emily, who stood in front of her desk against the urban Atlanta backdrop through the office window. Meghan's two colleagues sat nearby in the large office. The tasteful and comfortable décor invited clients to plan and consult about their important events.

"Yes, I've confirmed all the guests for the venues," Meghan told her. "For both dinners. That was the last thing I had to do. The Fink-Walton party as well. I'll go early to one to check everything then head to the other. At least they're near each other."

Emily's eyes crinkled with her smile. "Good job. I knew I could count on you. They'll have a great event, and you'll get some rest afterward."

Meghan forced a smile. If only that were true. After she went home that evening, she'd have completed the biggest projects for her event planning job for the spring. Marked off. Her caseload of early-May engagement, retirement, and rehearsal dinners would then give way to a short though welcome lull.

But Adam said he had news for her, and he'd tell her that weekend. Whether it was good or bad, she had no idea. His voice had given away nothing, so her fretfulness had been stuck in high gear since a few days ago when he'd left on a company trip. He hadn't called and had only texted once. Could she even look forward to a restful and romantic weekend? She braced for the worst.

Another thing hovered in her mind, her dad's mitral valve heart procedure the following week. It wasn't supposed to be too serious, but there was always a chance it was more than they thought. Or that he and his wife, Jill, were trying to protect her by playing down the dangers.

An hour later, Meghan slumped into the driver's seat of her car, almost too tired to start the ignition. She still had to attend the events, though not for the entire evening. Emily allowed the employees to leave work early on the days when they had evening events. She'd go home to rest and regroup. Then she'd have a clearer mind before heading out again.

Still no call from Adam, though she'd texted him. *Are you back yet? What, no news?* She regretted that after sending it. Sounded clingy. Needy and entitled. But they were a couple, weren't they? Was she being demanding just because she wanted him to act like it?

A glance at herself in her rearview mirror reflected dark, anxious eyes and a worried downturn of her lips, making her look older than her twenty-eight years. Even her stylish shoulder-length haircut looked exhausted and cranky.

The frown hung with her until she reached her garden-level apartment and unlocked the two deadbolts on the front door. As soon as light flooded the hall and living room, she kicked off her stiletto-heel pumps and removed her chunky necklace. She headed toward the lamp table in the kitchen cove.

Call her old-fashioned, but she had a backup landline on the table, in case of emergency. In case she lost her cell phone, or it somehow self-destructed. The phone blinked and hope flickered inside as she pushed *play*. When she heard Adam's voice, relief cascaded over her. His flight was delayed, and he wouldn't be in until late. So, he'd touch base the following day. He didn't say when. At least there was a reason, though she couldn't guess why he'd called her landline instead of her cell.

In bare feet, Meghan shuffled to the fridge. A peek inside met her low expectations. A lonely half-burrito from yesterday's dinner would have to do, unless she was able to sneak an hors d'oeuvre from a tray passing by at the dinner that evening.

Once heated, it did a passable job in dulling the growl in her stomach. She lay down for a rest, not to sleep, still scanning her list to make sure everything would be perfect for the evening.

Two hours later, Meghan headed out again, refueled to some degree by her brief rest and a fresh change of clothes. She'd completed most of the details in advance, as usual.

For bigger events, she worked in tandem with one of her colleagues. But an engagement party at a restaurant was relatively straightforward to plan compared to a multi-day conference. She and Emily had considered doing two in one evening doable because of the simpler format and the fact that the two restaurants were near each other. The previous day, she'd overseen the room setup for each venue, reviewed the program with the staff, and double-checked the seating and access. That evening, she only had to survey everything again with a careful eye at both venues.

Then go home to crash.

Her first stop was MacDowell's, an upscale steak restaurant with a large private dining room. Meghan greeted a few of the waiters who were still setting up. "Looks great, guys," she told them.

She turned toward the doorway as the bride, groom, and their parents entered. The Simmons-Burnett wedding party. The couple and their parents greeted Meghan.

The room grew noisy with six additional people.

"Everything looks great." The bride, a thirty-something brunette, addressed Meghan then shifted her gaze to her tall groom-to-be, seeming to forget Meghan's existence.

Meghan smiled as she felt herself grow invisible. A hollow breeze flowed through her. She'd had that once. Though not with Adam.

A noise in the hallway caused everyone to turn as two more couples came in, dressed in business casual and silky dresses. "We're a little early," the woman in three contrasting necklaces said. "We wanted to see the happy couple first." They glanced around, their smiles turning to confusion. "Where are Becky and Matt?"

"Becky and Matt who?" asked the bride's mother.

"We're here for the Fink-Walton wedding." One of the new arrivals, a man in a tweed sport coat, spoke up.

"This is the Simmons-Burnett wedding," Olivia Simmons said. "Are you all in the right place?"

As Meghan observed the exchange, a ripple of cold terror trickled through her. She blinked at the cluster of guests. "Wait." She approached them. "This is the venue for..." Her mouth dropped open. "Simmons-Burnett." Everyone fell silent and stared at Meghan. "Oh my gosh..."

She shot a stricken look at Olivia and her groom, Justin, whose mouths had fallen open. "I think I sent your guests to the wrong venue."

"You what?" Olivia's mother sputtered, her face turning a mottled pink.

Meghan stifled the urge to ball her fists to her ears and wail, *No, no, no!* She had to remain professional. And think fast.

"Stay calm, everyone." She gave her voice an authoritative edge as would a teacher of fifth graders, but added a reassuring smile. "Usually, everything goes like clockwork, but every once in a while, details get turned around."

She went to the two couples who'd just arrived. "There was a glitch in communication—my glitch, that is. Becky and Matt are at Goldman's, just across the highway. Do you know it?"

"I know the place," one of the men said. "It's not that far." He looked at his wife, who appeared relieved. "Good thing we came early."

Meghan turned to the bridal couple and their parents. The mother of the bride struggled to compose herself, looking like she wanted to tear Meghan's hair out. "It'll be fine, Mrs. Simmons. I really apologize for this. We have time to straighten it out." She kept her voice calm even as her heart pounded against her ribs like a mob of angry men locked in a basement. "I have a text list and an email list of all the guests for both parties. I'll notify them all immediately of the mistake and send them on to Goldmans."

"And what about *our* guests?" Olivia put her hands on her hips.

"I'll do the same for your list." Meghan swiped her tablet where she'd been double checking everything for weeks, hoping her calm demeanor would convince everyone things were still going to unfold smoothly, despite the mix-up. Having all the guests in a group mailing would be a lifesaver that evening.

After a few swipes and a lot of perspiration running down her back, she said, "Done. This will reroute all the guests in both parties. If anyone doesn't get the message in time, I'll let them know as soon as they arrive."

"What about the other guests? Will they know to come here?" The groom asked.

"I'll have someone there do the same. I'll call Goldman's now."

Meghan left the group to breathe deeply and have a quiet space. She phoned the manager of Goldman's. "Can you get him for me?" she asked the hostess who'd answered the phone. "It's urgent,"

She explained the mix-up and the man chuckled. He said, "It happens. I'll take care of them." His casual attitude sent Meghan a gust of relief, but the guests might be another story. Time would tell. They wouldn't necessarily let her know they received her message. She'd simply have to wait it out. And pray.

By the time all the guests were rerouted to their respective restaurants and bridal parties, both dinners ran late by thirty minutes. A few couples at each venue hadn't gotten the message and had to get back in the car. Some grumbled while others were more gracious. If the venues had been farther from each other, the whole evening would have been an unqualified catastrophe.

Meghan made an appearance at both restaurants, rushing from one to the other as a steady stream of panic surged through her veins. She addressed everyone's concerns, speaking soothingly instead of howling in shame. Fortunately, the event at Goldman's had a later start time, so she was able to take the microphone at the beginning of each event and apologize to everyone for the confusion. After doing the same at Goldman's, she slipped out of the restaurant and returned to her car. For the second time that day, she didn't immediately start the car, but stared through the windshield at a cluster of trees blackened by the night.

How had she done this? Had her anxiety with Adam, along with that of her father's upcoming surgery, thrown her off balance? She always double and triple checked everything, had always been known and praised for her organization and efficiency. The events were relatively simple, but there'd been many others which had competed with her mental bandwidth, resulting in an apparent overload of details.

What would Emily say? Word would surely get back, along with Meghan's own confession, which she'd make to her boss as soon as possible.

Emptied of strength, Meghan started her car and returned home, opened the door, and trudged in like an elderly woman. A layer of humiliation blended with dread of Emily's reaction hung on her shoulders like a tattered shawl. Despite her turmoil, she went to bed and fell into an exhausted sleep.

The following morning, Meghan awoke with a promising level of energy, until she remembered the debacle of the previous evening.

She'd failed and deserved to be fired. There was nothing to do, nothing to say. As she stared at the ceiling, she whispered a pathetic prayer. She'd ruined the engagement party for two different couples. Trashed the first phase of their happy futures together. And probably lost her job. No, she'd certainly lost it.

And here, she'd had visions of moving up in the company, eventually being entrusted with higher-level clients in a special, elite account only Emily handled.

Meghan had tried human resources, she'd tried bookkeeping, but event planning had been the sweet spot, the place where she belonged. Her organized mind and sociable nature fit right into that profession. Staying in the company would enable her to put all her vision and planning skills to higher and higher tests.

So much for *that* dream. At least, in her current company. What would she do now? Would she have to start from scratch? She could always try to get her old job back in Virginia, the one she had before fleeing to Atlanta...

She pulled herself from the bed, her limbs heavy like concrete. After brewing coffee, she collapsed on the couch and gazed at her phone. She should call Emily. But first, there was a message. Maybe Adam?

Not Adam. Emily.

"Meghan, I heard about what happened last night. I don't know how it happened, and won't be able to discuss it until Monday. We'll look at it then. Sounds like everything went okay afterward, but I was surprised, because you're usually such a perfectionist. We'll talk about this on Monday."

Meghan couldn't discern from Emily's tone if she was frustrated or even ready to fire Meghan. She'd be forced to wait until Monday. Until then, she'd scour the internet for job openings.

On top of everything else, Adam still hadn't called. He could be tired from his late flight, and would call her later. But over the last month or two, making excuses for Adam had become her new hobby. She was tired of guessing the reasons for his recent lukewarm attitude, his failure to respond in a minimum of ways.

She'd met Adam at a training workshop for social media, one offered to local companies in various disciplines. Emily had wanted her to receive more training in that area, since she was not only lousy at it, but disinterested. Yet, in her industry and many others, it was essential, so she decided to go and learn to like it. During a coffee break, Adam introduced himself, then later sought her out during the lunch break. He did the same the following day, which led to a date. That was six months ago.

Her gaze found the wall clock. Almost ten o'clock. Wouldn't he be up?

She tapped his number, knowing better, since it was his place to call her. But she needed a friendly voice. No, that wasn't the first thing she needed. She wanted reassurance, as well as a distraction from her failures at work. His number rang four times. Then a woman's voice answered. "Adam's phone. Who's this?"

Meghan froze. The words, *his girlfriend, who are you?* ricocheted inside her brain.

Instead, she disconnected.

ও ও ও

Luc Badaux clicked *purchase ticket* then leaned back in his chair with a long sigh. Whatever his misgivings about flying to Chicago for a few days, it was still his mom's sixtieth birthday. She'd be thrilled by his visit, and that was worth all the inconvenience. It was even worth putting up with Dad.

His gaze wandered through the tall plate-glass window of the fourteenth-floor building where he worked. The flat landscape stretched out to a dry, steamy horizon. Flat, lifeless. No green for miles, except a few intentionally landscaped puffs neatly spaced apart on the street far below. He could only imagine the sizzling West Texas sun outside. A few days up north would be a pleasant break, wouldn't it?

After a year and a half in the Lone Star state, Luc hadn't grown accustomed to the moon-like landscape and the furnace of heat in spring and summer. He hadn't grown up there and had never learned to appreciate its uniqueness the same way the natives did.

Face it, you made a mistake coming here. He let out a humorless chuckle. Roughly one week after his arrival to work in his so-called dream job at a tech startup, that sad truth had hit home.

His blunder in judgment had entwined a more devastating mistake, one he'd spent the last year trying to expunge from his mind. He'd tried to call her, to backpedal, but nothing he said would erase his error. On top of that, she'd blocked his number.

"You losing concentration, Frenchy?" Luc's office mate, David, rose to get a can of Coke from the small fridge in the corner of their sunlit office.

"Don't call me Frenchy, Redneck." But Luc was smiling. At least he got along well with David, which was more than he could say for the rest of his team. "Or else I'll have to curse you out in French. It'll sound pretty, but believe me, it won't be."

David guffawed. "Tough talk. Go eat a croissant, will ya?"

Luc laughed. He'd been taking that kind of teasing for most of his life in the US, though usually it was good-natured. He'd spent his first twelve years in the South of France with his French father and American mother. Then his dad got a new job in suburban Chicago. Luc gradually became fully Americanized. On most days. He could easily put on an authentic French accent if it suited his purpose. And he still craved plenty of things he'd left behind. The French pace of life, the sing-song music of the Provence accent. And his grandma Isabelle, who he'd always called *Mamie*.

He should go back to see her. She was almost ninety and frail. He didn't know how long she'd last after her winter bout with pneumonia. Hard to believe his sweet, pillowy grandmother had raised his obnoxious, irascible dad.

Back to work. He had a lot to do if he was to be caught up enough to take off time next week to fly to Chicago.

Chapter Two

Meghan trudged into the office on Monday morning, dread oozing out of each of her pores. She hadn't spoken to Emily over the weekend, understanding clearly that her boss didn't want to address the restaurant fiasco until Monday.

Monday, execution day. The day she'd lose her job. And she deserved it.

She didn't wait for Emily to summon her, but hovered outside her boss's door until the woman finished her phone call, sending urgent prayers heavenward while she waited. Emily gestured her in with a flick of her fingers and Meghan dutifully sat across the wide glass desktop from her. She swallowed the lump in her throat and before she could begin apologizing, tears stung her eyes. She blinked them away, but didn't trust herself to speak.

"Hey, Meghan. You're looking pretty miserable." Emily folded her hands on the desk and spoke in a gentle voice. "It's not the end of the world."

Her tone surprised Meghan, who raised her gaze, glazed with tears. She blinked again. "I messed up *two* engagement parties."

Emily leaned back with a humored twist on her lips. "At least the two venues weren't that far from each other."

Meghan nodded. "That saved the evening. But what if your company gets bad reviews because of me?"

Emily shrugged. "Oh well."

"You're not yelling at me. Aren't you angry?" Meghan pressed her lips together, sure something else was coming.

"I'm not yelling because it's not my style, as you know. It all worked out and some people found it humorous, according to one of the brides, who told me about it. I'm not saying I'm glad it happened. But whatever damage control you did worked. The brides themselves seemed understanding. One of the mothers, less so, but that's how the mothers often are."

"You're not going to fire me?"

Emily smiled. "No, I'm not."

Relief flooded through Meghan. "Really?"

"Really. Meghan, I know your work ethic. I figured something was going on with you at a personal level. And I know from experience people make mistakes when they haven't taken a vacation in—" She glanced down at a jotted note on her desktop. "Since you got here, in fact. You've worked here for a year, and you've never taken time off. If you recall, you held down the fort last summer while I had my surgery, even though you were a new hire."

"Yes, I remember. I didn't take off because it was only my first year. And everything's always so…busy."

Aside from that, she'd still been recovering from the chief romantic disaster of her young life *and* a move to a new state. She hadn't even known anyone back then to socialize with, so she worked. And worked. While she grieved.

"And it always will be, hopefully. But that doesn't mean you don't get a life. Are there other pressures going on you feel like sharing? You don't have to tell me, of course."

"No, I don't mind. I broke up with my boyfriend over the weekend. We'd been together for over six months and things weren't going well for the last month or so. He…he was cheating on me. And then there's my dad, who's having heart surgery in a few days."

"I see." Emily folded her hands on her desk, as if she had all the time in the world. "So, you've had a great deal of pressure recently and almost no time off in a year."

Meghan met Emily's compassionate gaze as a smile pulled at her lips. "You're being so kind. I don't deserve it."

"Nonsense. It sounds like to me you just need a break to clear your head and remember that everything's okay. You still have a job, and I have some more work for you. Don't worry. But there is one thing I will require you to do."

"Name it." Meghan straightened in her chair.

"I want you to take two weeks of vacation."

"Two? I think a few days is all I'll need—"

"Two. No less. If you need more, that's fine too. I need to be sure you're rested before the summer rolls in. It's the perfect time, really, because the summer events have been scheduled, but won't ramp up until after you're back. And I have other competent people, don't forget."

True, Meghan wasn't indispensable, nor irreplaceable. She'd learned that lesson early and well.

"Okay. If that's your requirement, I accept." She smiled then. Paid time off instead of a pink slip. "When should I take off?"

"As soon as possible. How is Friday? You're caught up on the big things, I believe. I'll give new accounts to Chelsea and Lynn while you're gone. So, you can take the next few days to tie up any loose ends, then disappear. I don't want to see your face in here for at least two weeks."

Meghan almost cried at Emily's benevolence. She rose. "I'll get right to tying up loose ends. Thank you, Emily."

"Remember, Meghan. Everyone makes mistakes. Sounds like a cliché, but it's true. I've made them. Everyone has. Your job is important, of course, but it *is* just a job."

Meghan nodded and left the woman's office with the sensation of having received a huge gift.

ଓ ଓ ଓ

Luc scanned the rows of cars as they pulled along the curb, then away at O'Hare Airport in Chicago. He shifted his weight against a small suitcase and entertained himself people-watching. Hugs, laughter, people rushing, lots of luggage. Finally, he spied the silver Mustang belonging to his brother, Max. He waved in Max's direction, seeing his wavy dark hair through the windshield. Max pulled to the curb and wedged between two other cars before hopping out.

The brothers exchanged a hug and Max grabbed Luc's suitcase. "How was your flight?" he asked once they were on their way.

"Standard question." Luc grinned. "Standard answer. Fine."

Max laughed. "Now we've got that out of the way. How's Texas?"

Luc shrugged. "I'm getting away from it this weekend, so we can't talk about that either. I'm sure there are nice parts. Greener with landscapes. I just don't happen to live there."

His brother snorted. "Come back here. Lots of green in the suburbs. Lots of jobs for a techie like you too."

"Whatever." Max was right. Luc could easily get a job there, if that's what he wanted. Of course, he couldn't do that yet. He liked his work, but a lot of other elements were missing in his life. He didn't feel like talking about that with Max or anyone else, including himself.

So much of it came down to *her*. The one he'd let get away, or rather, the one he'd inadvertently left behind. After her, nothing had been the same. Though it was over a year ago, she hovered in his subconscious and sometimes even showed up in his dreams. A bad and good memory all at once.

But this weekend was about his mom. And reconnecting with his childhood home and with Max, who lived only twenty minutes away in another town.

Two years his junior, Max was the one person in Luc's family he could call a friend. They had little news to exchange that day because they talked weekly by text or phone. And sometimes watched French soccer matches streamed on their TVs as they shared the experience by computer. Fortunately, Luc lived alone, since those matches could get raucous.

Max knew more than anyone how much Luc regretted his decision to move to Texas. He'd hid his discontent from his mother, who hadn't been in favor of the move in the first place. Because of *her*, of course. The startup he worked for wasn't as glamorous and cutting edge as Luc had been led to believe. But he'd only been there eighteen months. Too soon to look for something else, according to his professional timetable.

Luc shot a glance at Max. "How's Mom?"

"She's good. She always is when you come. I think you're her favorite."

"Yeah, of course. And with good reason."

They laughed.

No one mentioned Dad. Luc would deal with him soon enough. Max didn't have the same experience with their dad as Luc did, being a different personality type with a different profession. Luc was the firstborn, and to make matters worse, was similar in aptitudes, though not temperament, to his dad. Maybe that's why they often butted heads. It was a truth Luc had to recognize and swallow. Like a bad-tasting pill.

Thirty minutes later, they pulled into the driveway of the familiar two-story home where Luc had spent his childhood, from age twelve to eighteen, when he'd left for college. Now he was thirty years old, and it looked small and worn to him. His parents ought to downsize or at least do some renovations.

They entered the house. "Hello?" called Max.

Luc nudged Max and gestured toward the dining room, which looked freshly painted in pale yellow. "Didn't the walls used to be faded flowered paper?"

"Yeah, they started renovating the house. Room by room. Guess you haven't been here in a while."

A twinge of guilt sailed through Luc's chest. True. He hadn't made it up the previous Christmas. Made some excuse he could no longer remember. His workload always served as a plausible pretext for whatever he didn't want to do. "Glad they're renovating. It was long overdue." Though his mom *had* talked about it on the phone.

"Oh, you're here!" Luc heard his mom's voice float toward them from the kitchen. She appeared in the hall, a smile stretched across her face. Additional lines he hadn't noticed before webbed from her eyes and she looked shorter. Older. They exchanged hugs, and she held him tight, as if afraid to let him go.

"The dining room looks better." Luc gestured with a nod toward the room. "What else have you guys done?" She must have described the various projects on the phone over the last few months, but he'd been too distracted to retain the details. More guilt boomeranged inside.

"I'll show you what we've done to this point after we have something to drink. *And* eat." She led the way to the kitchen where the nutty smells of roasted sugar and chocolate filled the air, making his mouth water.

"I made monster cookies, the ones you loved as a child."

Luc licked his lips. "You didn't have to do that, Mom. But I won't refuse."

She set a plate of big cookies, still steaming and studded with chocolate, nuts, and coconut, on the table. His mom always added coconut to the traditional recipe because Luc loved it. "I wanted to celebrate your visit."

"But it's *your* birthday." Luc didn't wait to be invited. He reached for a still-warm cookie. "Thanks for these. Mmm." Smooth, warm chocolate coated his throat. Pure pleasure alongside poignant memories. For sure, he had the best of both worlds, the French and the American. A double set of delicacies to savor, places to visit, people, and traditions.

She gave the plate a little push toward him. "My birthday isn't big news. I get one every year." She smiled. "The renovations are going slowly because your father's been working a lot, and I don't like to supervise all these people by myself. Though I have had to learn to some degree."

"But you're happy with the results." Max finally spoke through a mouthful of cookies.

"Yes, it's a big difference. We'd talked about moving, but decided to renovate instead. I'm starting to like the house again. Why don't you settle into your old room with your stuff, Luc?"

He shot her a playful look. "Will I recognize it?"

"Yes, I'm pretty sure you will. I didn't redo it in pink ruffles or anything. Don't worry."

He chuckled and picked up his bag.

"After that, I'll show you the den and the master bedroom," she called after him as he started up the staircase. "They're all finished. Your dad'll be home soon, and we'll do some chicken on the grill."

Luc made appropriate noises of approval as his mother led him on a tour of the renovations.

When his dad came home, they exchanged a brief hug. "It's been a while since your last visit."

Luc didn't know if that was a rebuke or an observation, and wouldn't look too deep into it.

"Work going alright?" Fabrice Badaux pulled a cold beer from the fridge. He popped the top from the can. When they moved to the States years earlier, his father had adapted his name into an American *Bryce*, which he'd kept ever since. Hadn't ever really fit him, though. At sixty-four, his dad still had a full head of hair laced with silver, and a direct blue-eyed gaze that matched the hardness of his personality. He'd never lost his French accent, though twenty years of life and business dealings in the States had diluted it to what some considered a charming level.

"Yeah, fine. Can't really add much. It's busy." He didn't want to go into detail about his projects with his programmer father, who would certainly understand the content, but lack interest. No point in going there.

Luc exchanged a look with Max. He also wouldn't share his current low job satisfaction with either of his parents. His mom would urge him to find something else and not let up until he did. His dad would say, *You should have let me set you up with something here. I have lots of connections ...*

He wasn't ready to hear either one. He'd figure it out on his own.

After Fabrice cooked marinated chicken breasts on the grill, the four of them ate dinner around the patio table on the deck. A ring of mature trees encircled the backyard where Luc and Max had endlessly kicked a soccer ball back in the day. All the bare places had filled in with lush bushes and flowers his mother had planted and lovingly cared for over the years. It felt surprisingly peaceful to be back there on such familiar turf. He should visit more often. It had even crossed his mind to one day move back, though he'd have to find a way to limit his exposure to his dad, with whom he'd never learned to get along.

Luc's dad went inside for another beer and returned outside. "I saw Freddie Harmon the other day." He settled into his chair. "He's a casual friend who has a business involving video and other types of media. He was telling me he wants to expand the online aspect and include a range of AI tools and capabilities." He directed his gaze at Luc. "He's looking for a programmer of your experience to expand his business. We talked about it a little and I told him I'd mention it to you. He works in Chicago. Maybe he'd let you work remotely once you were familiar with everything. Your mother would love to have you around more."

Luc wiped his mouth with a paper napkin, hesitant to respond. At that moment, he had to admit, the idea was appealing. Cool Illinois rather than broiling Texas. Closer to the home about which he'd just had a wave of nostalgia, not that he put much stock in that. But he didn't want to look too eager. He'd talk to the guy, Freddie, and find out more. "How soon is he looking to fill the position?"

"I don't know. He just talked to me about it. Sounds like he just started working on the job description, so it's wide open. You should talk to him."

"Yeah, I will. See what's involved." And not make the same mistake he'd made moving to Texas for the so-called dream job. The balmy breeze of that spring night made him want to ask how soon he could move and start the new job. Something inside simmered. Interest? Definitely.

"Might be nice to live in a cooler place than Texas," he finally said.

"Is that the only reason to move back home?" His mother frowned, hurt displayed in her eyes.

Luc gave her a wide grin and reached across the table to squeeze her hand. "Of course not, Mom. Being nearby would be perfect. Not home, of course. I'd get my own place."

Mollified, she squeezed his hand back and offered a smile. "My world would be complete."

"Laying it on a bit thick, Mom." Luc winked at her, and she laughed.

"You could live with me until you get settled, depending on where this place is," Max said.

Luc held up a hand. "Okay, slow down everyone. It's an interesting idea, but I need to hear more about the job. I'll only say I'm not *closed* to the idea of changing jobs, and it might be nice to be back in this area. But one thing at a time."

"I'll have Freddie give you a call." Luc's father reached for a cornbread muffin.

"No, I'd rather contact him myself. Give me his email and phone number. And the name of his company. I'll look it up online first to see what he does. I'll see from that if it could be a fit." He'd know pretty quickly from the website if it would be worth it to go farther. But he'd still talk to the guy. Freddie.

"Don't forget to tell him I sent you. Freddie and I go way back." His father raised his eyebrows in a deliberate stare.

"I'm pretty sure I can talk to him on my own. I've been in this type of work a long time. And if you've already talked to him about me, there's no need. I'll just tell him I'm...how we're related." Somehow the word *son* had always stuck in his throat when he described his relationship with his dad.

His dad didn't seem to notice. "It can't hurt to have an inside connection. He said he wants to talk to you if you're interested. I didn't know if you'd be ready to change jobs this soon or not."

Luc took a breath. His dad made it sound like he jumped from job to job. He'd been in his position in Virginia for four years. "I'm not necessarily ready to look for something else, but it won't hurt to talk to him." No need to explain that he'd love a way out of Texas and invite more pressure from his entire family.

"I told him my boy takes after his old man." His dad chuckled.

"Huh. What did you mean by that?"

"We have the same profession, same interests." His dad shrugged, seeming oblivious to the way he pushed Luc's buttons.

Irritation simmered inside him. "It's not like I'm a mirror image of you, Dad, just because we're both in IT." He couldn't stop himself from adding, "Or as you like to think, a paler version of yourself." Luc took a swig of sparkling water. He knew he sounded like a snotty kid, but had been hearing things like that from his dad his whole life. "Don't flatter yourself so much."

His dad looked surprised and displeased. "You don't think I inspired you somehow in your choice of profession?"

"No, not at all." Luc's jaw hardened. "We're wired the same way intellectually, but that doesn't mean I resemble you in any other way."

What a stupid conversation. But it wasn't the first time. His dad was so full of himself, he somehow took credit for the fact that Luc excelled in the same domain and ended up in the same profession. All his life, Luc had never had his own spotlight. His own accomplishments or validation. It was all about Dad, the center of the Badaux family, the center of his universe.

Luc couldn't do much about his penchant for all things technical. He loved it and wasn't willing to sacrifice that in order to be more dissimilar to his dad. But in every other area, he pursued differences. He tried everything to distinguish himself, seeking anything that was opposite from what his dad liked. In some things, he succeeded. In others, like a boomerang, he found himself back in the same place as his dad.

Fabrice liked to think of Luc as his mirror image for the sake of his own ego. Luc had been trying to break the mirror for thirty years.

Chapter Three

What would she do for two weeks?

The question both intrigued and intimidated Meghan as she settled against the fluffy pillow on her couch. She'd shed her work clothes and downed a grain bowl she'd brought from her favorite Asian takeout place.

A giddy but unfamiliar sense of lightness invaded her as she considered the reality that she *did* still have a job, but was being *ordered* to take a vacation. A win-win. It felt foreign to her, after a year of pressure, during which she hadn't dared think of even a long weekend away, let alone two weeks.

But she still had to address the matter. What would she do? Where would she go? Going home was out of the question, since she hadn't had a home in a long time, a fact that carved a hollow place inside her. Not since her parents had split up, and each went off and created new homes of their own.

Well, that was one way to think of it. Several years ago, when Meghan was in her early twenties, her mother left the marriage after falling in love, she'd claimed, with another instructor at the same college where she and Meghan's father worked. She and her husband, Bert, still lived in northern Virginia, but in a different suburb from the one where Meghan had grown up. After the divorce, her dad eventually remarried too, then took an early retirement in Myrtle Beach. And he'd be recovering from heart surgery at the very time she needed to be on vacation.

So no, home wasn't an option. She was close with her dad, but cordial was the best she could manage with her mother, whose betrayal of the family was lodged in Meghan's chest like a slab of concrete.

Then, there were her twin sisters, Jenn and Mia, six years older. They lived across the country and had their own lives, into which they never invited Meghan. Same as during her childhood. Meghan had grown up like an only child due to the age gap, since she'd been a later arrival, an unplanned pregnancy. At the time, she didn't understand why she was often excluded by her sisters. The pain of being left out trailed her into adolescence, at which point she determined she didn't need them anyway.

When Meghan was seven, she overheard her mother tell a friend on the phone that Meghan had been an *accident*. That word lodged like a dagger in her heart until, with maturity, she understood better. She never doubted her parents' love for her, but the knowledge of her being *unplanned* whispered cruel taunts from time to time, making her wonder if she truly belonged in her family. Add to that her sisters' treatment, as though she *didn't* belong. Another story better left on the shelf where it gathered dust and stale hurt.

Staying in her own apartment for two weeks didn't attract her either, although she ought to stay and clean every surface and closet. She'd likely end up depressed, even though she'd have a sparkling apartment to show for it.

That was certainly not what Emily had in mind with her mandated vacation time. A trip would be necessary, but where? Meghan snagged her phone from the coffee table and texted her best friend, Shane, who still lived in Virginia. *I've been ordered to take two weeks' vacation starting this Friday. Is there any place you'd like to travel with me? Give me some ideas!*

A few minutes later, the response came with a musical beep. *A great idea, but too short notice. I have some deadlines hanging over my head and my parents' anniversary party coming up. If you can wait till July, it's a go.*

Meghan frowned. Of course, it was short notice. No one could just up and go unless they were retired and bored. She knew no one in that camp, and if she did, how much fun would they be on a trip? Going to see Shane at her place for two weeks wasn't ideal either. *No, I can't wait. I'm on leave as of this Friday. We'll do it another time.* Frown emoji. *I'll just have to send you a postcard from...wherever.*

Sounds like there's a story behind this, though I must say, I'm glad you're finally taking time off. I want the details when you have time. Confused emoji.

The messy details? Okay (sigh) you'll get them. I'll call before I leave town (though not yet sure where.) Hope all is well with you.

She'd just have to go somewhere by herself. She didn't relish traveling alone, even though female solo travel had been quite popular for a while. This time, she wouldn't have a choice.

Meghan heaved herself off the couch and brought her laptop from the bedroom. For the next hour, she searched and surfed travel blogs and websites, scoping for inspiration—anything that might seize her interest enough to actually book an airline ticket. A cruise? An all-inclusive in the Caribbean? She might find a great deal on a last-minute booking with a company trying to fill their last spots.

Finally, she shut the laptop and relaxed against the cushion. Where had she gone in the past that she'd loved? And could she *return* to that treasured spot?

Postcard from Nice   *Kyle Hunter*

A fuzzy image of lemon-yellow Italianate architecture baking under lazy Provence sunshine fluttered into her mind. Nice, France. Yes, that was it. Along with the image came a faint ache. She'd been there with Luc. Though her memory included the source of her heartache, she couldn't deny the magic of the place.

Meghan closed her eyes and imagined the corner fifth-story apartment with its wrap-around porch. They'd had breakfast on the porch each day, a light breeze stirring the awning as the neighborhood awakened. There were two bedrooms, so they'd behaved. But evenings on the porch or strolling hand-in-hand through the lively plazas under the mimosa trees had oozed romance, hope, and promises. She'd fallen in love with him in Nice. At least back then, she was protected from the crushing events that would follow only a few months later.

Could she stay in that same apartment? How she'd love to spend evenings on the same corner balcony watching the setting sun as lights sparkled from nearby buildings. Just beyond, a distant view of the Mediterranean Sea, and the soulful cry of seagulls overhead. She could nearly smell the salty air, hear the cadence of French conversations on the streets below.

Luc owned the apartment, an early inheritance from his grandmother Isabelle, but an agency managed it. He'd never even know Meghan was staying there. He'd chosen his faraway life in Texas, so her secret would be safe. Would a two-week visit in the same apartment flood her with memories of Luc and undo her progress getting over him? It might, but a trip to Nice was already simmering in her mind. And once an idea took hold in Meghan's head, it was nearly impossible to dislodge it. Her mother used to call her a force of nature. A strength and weakness all at once.

Was the apartment even available? That would be a stretch, especially at short notice during the month of May. If it was already booked, she'd stay somewhere else. Even though it had been nearly two years, she remembered the agency's name, probably because Luc had complained about it several times during their visit. Pierrot Maisons de Vacances. Hopefully, the apartment was listed with the same agency.

Meghan reopened her laptop and pulled up the Pierrot website. She scanned the current available offerings. The apartment was still there. Her gaze roved through a small gallery of photos, which matched her memories of that summer. Anticipation fluttered inside like a swarm of hummingbirds. She inserted the date. It was available! She remembered

Luc saying the place was often booked six months or more in advance. Was she receiving divine guidance, open doors? *Thank you, Lord!* Maybe it was meant to be.

Two weeks in Nice. It would cost her, but it would be worth it. And she couldn't think of any other place she wanted to go for two weeks. She inserted her credit card number and clicked *Book*. Minutes later, the confirmation popped into her inbox. No turning back.

Now she only hoped she'd have a wonderful vacation without being haunted by memories of tender moments with Luc. Luc, who'd later broken her heart by taking a job in Texas without even consulting her. They'd been together nearly a year, and she hadn't even known he was interviewing. He'd insisted he hadn't searched, but a headhunter had offered him his dream job. His actions loudly proclaimed how little she meant to him. She wasn't part of his job considerations or his future picture. His career was primary, and always would be, as his uber-diligent work habits had often demonstrated. Work first. *Him* first. Never her. He'd simply left her out, left her behind.

She ought to be used to it by now.

Unbidden, her thoughts meandered to the day they met. She'd been hired in human resources at a company in northern Virginia where he'd already worked in IT for a few years. When he'd told her his name, Luc Badaux, she'd giggled.

Badd-O? Like Bad Dough? Or should I just call you Bad Boy?

He'd rolled his eyes as if he'd heard that one too many times. *Badaux, like Bordeaux.* His voice had been stiff.

She'd been mesmerized by his accent, the percussive way he'd pronounced *daux*. Nothing like Dough. *And your name is Luke?*

He shook his head. *Luc.* His pronunciation was decidedly different from hers. And the way he puckered his lips when he pronounced the vowel stayed in her mind. For a long time. And frequently visited her imagination.

How about if I just call you Lucky?

Not sure that applies, he'd said, deadpan. Then he'd frowned, looking put out, irritated by her antics. He didn't seem up for joking around, but rather looked bored with the exchange. *Just call me Luke.* Then he dismissed her, as if she were an annoying cousin. Probably thought she was some idiot girl who'd never traveled, knew nothing of accents and foreign names. From then on, she seldom conversed with him, but sometimes called him *Bad Boy*, which he hadn't liked.

It had started out as immature fun on her part, especially since he seemed to prickle with her teasing. That is, until it started roiling between them, with heated stares and sarcastic quips that hid a smoldering attraction, one that took on a life of its own.

This continued for several months. Then one Friday evening there was a company-wide retirement party at a local restaurant for the vice-president of the company. Fifty or so employees filled a private dining room, enjoying a catered meal, along with the opportunity to approach a microphone to praise, roast, tease, and give well wishes to the guest of honor.

Luc sat across the room from Meghan at a different table. Throughout the meal, her awareness of him distracted her like a persistent mosquito. Though she tried to engage in conversation with those at her table, her attention repeatedly rebounded across the room to Luc. She was impossibly attracted to him, and had no idea what to do about it.

Instead, she attempted to avoid looking at him, but a force stronger than her decision drew her gaze across the room, often meeting his.

Toward the end of the evening, Meghan rose to go to the restrooms, located down a short hallway in another part of the restaurant. As she washed her hands, she took a deep breath. Her feelings were getting out of hand. At least she worked in a different part of the building from Luc and could usually avoid him.

When she exited the restroom, she stopped. Luc stood about two feet away, facing her in the semi-darkness of the hallway. For a suspended moment, their gazes locked and neither said a word, but a tornado of chemistry might as well be whirling around them.

Without a word, he stepped toward her, grasped her face, and kissed her. After a split-second of shock, she responded by circling her arms around his waist and pressing into him. Passion and built-up desire wrapped hungry tentacles around both of them, as his lips covered hers, exploring, probing. Moments later, without releasing her, he pulled his head back far enough to stare into her eyes. He'd whispered, *Was I wrong about this?* She mutely shook her head.

Dinner? Tomorrow? She nodded in response with a breathy *yes* before he eased her toward the wall and kissed her again. Then he stepped back to let her pass, as if nothing had happened, but his eyes were dark with promise.

Thinking about that day caused perspiration to break out on Meghan's back and neck and she pulled off her sweater, then shook the picture from her mind. As if she could.

☙ ☙ ☙

Meghan should have been sleepy after little rest on the direct overnight flight from Atlanta. But her senses had come alive and percolated with sounds and sights. A tram rumbling by, snippets of French conversations, sweeping mimosa and plane trees lining the square.

At her feet sat her large suitcase and carry-on bag. And over her head loomed the six-story apartment building on Rue Cassini near Garibaldi Square, pale yellow with stately wrought-iron balconies and pert white shutters at each window. On either end of the building, palm trees caressed the sky, whispering as the breeze rustled their fronds, casting large orbs of shade along the sidewalks. Her eyes swept every inch of the building as she waited for the property manager, Sébastien, to arrive and give her the key.

The sight of it released a flood of memories, but not painful ones. Though she and Luc hadn't worked out, the mental snapshots of her idyllic moments there were like a secret treasure to be remembered but not kept. Like a beautiful sandcastle washed away by waves.

"Mademoiselle Clark?"

A man's voice broke into her reverie. Sébastien, a trim fiftyish man with a gray mustache, approached her on the sidewalk.

"Bonjour, I'm Miss Clark."

He shook her hand, grabbed the large suitcase, and led the way into the building. Thankfully, there was an elevator which rose to the fifth floor while Sébastien chatted with her. When he unlocked the apartment, her heart pounded against her ribs as anticipation and apprehension filled her.

She stepped inside. It looked the same as two years earlier, according to her cloudy memory, except for a new area rug and an updated armchair. But the feeling was the same. The same, except that Luc wasn't there. She was alone.

After a few cursory explanations about the apartment, Sébastian left. Meghan gazed around her, expecting to be flooded with painful memories. But there was more comfort and anticipation than trauma.

She explored each room, finding them mostly as she remembered, and left her suitcase in one of the bedrooms. The same dining table occupied a corner near the kitchen, and a spacious living room spread out on the other side. Behind it lay a short hallway with some closets, both bedrooms, a bathroom, and a tiny room, the *toilette* with a minuscule sink. Precisely *perfect* for her vacation.

Then the balcony...her favorite. She passed through the galley kitchen to the tall French doors. She flung them open, allowing light and city noise to flood into the space. Once on the balcony, cooler air fingered her hair and stroked her neck. At the railing, she looked out and looked down. It felt like home. Her temporary home. An outdoor table and four chairs still occupied one end. She'd have breakfast there, as she and Luc had done.

During that golden week they'd had together, Luc had been carefree. Nothing like when they were back in normal life in Virginia. There, it had been hard to compete with his emergency work projects and deadlines. Often, she'd felt squeezed into his life, which hurt more than she admitted.

But the week they'd spent in Nice, he'd been relaxed, charming, and attentive. He'd been the perfect boyfriend, romantic and focused. He'd also been the perfect tour guide, having grown up near there. Day by day, he'd slipped deeper into his French cultural self. She'd enjoyed watching it unfold before her, there on his turf. And she'd felt herself pulled toward him and more in love with him, a powerful force she couldn't resist.

Meghan sighed. A lovely memory with a crash ending.

Back to the present. She'd push aside the memories, good and bad, and explore her new temporary neighborhood. Meghan closed the balcony doors and took the elevator to the ground level. Once outside, she fished in her purse for the city map she'd picked up at a tourist office near the train station. It would fill the gaps in her recollections.

Nearby was the lively Garibaldi Square, where she could find lunch at one of several bustling bistros lined up under a canopy of mimosa trees. After that, she'd wander to the Old Town and browse the shops to stave off getting too sleepy from her flight.

Her imposed vacation had begun.

ര ര ര

In retrospect, Luc's weekend hadn't been too bad, aside from a few tense moments with his dad, who'd carelessly stirred a lifetime of frustration like a dormant hornet's nest. His mom had been delighted with all the fanfare the family put together around her birthday. Luc enjoyed seeing Max, as always.

A few relatives on his mom's side who didn't live too far also came. Seeing them again was more pleasant than he'd expected, though it was like making acquaintance with strangers. Might not be too bad to move back up north, to be around Max more. To look out the window and see green again.

His mom would be thrilled. He could even find a way to deal with his dad. The prospect had gone from impossible to appealing. Such a shift in one weekend.

His dad had given him Freddie's website and phone number, but with all the festivities, preparations, and family time, he hadn't had time to even look at it. At the airport, while he waited for his flight back to Texas, he'd had a few minutes to skim it. Curiosity turned into a thread of interest as he read the details of the company and the work they did. He'd gotten home too late to call Freddie, but sometime that day he'd take a moment to send the man an initial email expressing his interest, and ask a few questions. The new prospect might help him dig up his lost optimism.

For now, a boatload of work awaited him after his long weekend away. He'd be there late or else take it home, though taking work home was the norm. May as well scan his emails before diving into the current project. Anyone of immediate importance usually sent text messages, but not everyone. His eyes narrowed on the list filling his inbox, lighting on the name *Julien*. He tensed. Julien only communicated by email, likely because he didn't have an international calling plan.

Julien was a kind of uncle, though more of a close family friend. He lived in Villefranche-sur-

Mer, a town on the Mediterranean close to Luc's grandmother. Julien kept an eye on her, making sure she got her meals delivered and all her medical aides lined up. There must be bad news. Luc clicked on the mail.

Salut, Luc. I thought you should know that your grandmother has taken a turn, and she probably doesn't have a long time. She told me she wanted to see you. Will you be able to come to France soon?

Sadness welled up inside Luc. Snapshots of summers with his *Mamie,* as he'd always called her, filled his mind. Her *tarte tatin*, her warm hugs, her stories of her life as a child during the war. The previous year, he'd gone with Max to see her. During that visit, she'd signed over her second apartment to them. According to French inheritance laws, they'd pay less tax on it if she gave it to them while she was still alive. Along with the one in Nice she'd given to Luc, it was rented out for most of the year, and both provided a tidy side income. If he kept up the strategy, he wouldn't even have to work.

But then, for some reason, he was still driven. Trying to prove something, to himself, to the old man. Luc snorted. Why bother? Yet wasn't that the reason he'd abandoned the woman he loved to pursue the so-called dream job? He snorted again, causing David to raise his brows. Luc grimaced. The joke was on him.

I'm sorry to hear this, Julien. Of course, I'll come as soon as I can. I have to take off work, but I'll come. Is she still at home? Please keep me posted on the situation. Hope you are doing well. And give her my love.

Before pushing send, he thought of his dad, who'd fallen out with his mother a few years ago. He couldn't remember the reason. Would Julien have contacted him too? Probably. He added to the email, *Will you let Dad know?* That way, Luc wouldn't have to bear the bad news to his father. But would he come to her deathbed? Not likely.

Overall, a bland note, but how could he convey in an email what felt like stones lodged in his throat at the thought of losing his *Mamie*? He'd known this day was coming soon, of course. He'd ask Max to come, though it was unlikely he'd be able. He owned a bike shop and had just begun to franchise.

He shut his eyes for a moment and sent a silent prayer for his grandmother, who'd been a rock, a friend, and so much more. His spiritual mother, even. Any faith he had was thanks to her, and despite his natural skepticism about many things, he stubbornly hung onto his bumpy relationship with God. Lately, more bumps than usual, and his lethargy in finding a new church in Texas didn't help that domain of his life.

He took a moment to text Max and tell him the news, then emailed Sébastien, his property manager in Nice. *Hi Séb, I'll be coming for a week or two to see my grandmother, who's at the end of her life. Is the Cassini apartment available by chance? If not, is Riquier available? Please let me know as soon as you can. Otherwise, I'll have to rent something or stay with a friend. Thanks.*

Luc worked like a machine through the morning, catching up and keeping his grief under wraps. At noon, he saw a response from Sébastien. Cassini was rented. Riquier was available, and he'd given the dates. Good, at least he wouldn't have to rent something or pile in on Julien. He returned a note asking him to hold Riquier for him. Then he went to his boss's office.

"Did you have a good trip?" The man asked with a friendly smile.

"Yeah, it was nice to see everyone. My mom's sixtieth. Uh, I have another family-related request. I got a message over the weekend from France. My grandmother is close to dying and wants to see me. I...I'd like to see her before she's gone."

The man paused, as if thinking. Or deciding how to refuse. "Would a week or two help?"

A wave of relief washed over Luc. He hadn't expected a harsh response or refusal, but he'd just been out of the office less than a week ago. "Yes, that would help. I could even work remotely if I need more than a week."

"Sure, no problem. You'll have to leave soon, then, I assume."

"Yes. As soon as I can get a flight."

His boss nodded. "I'm sorry about your grandmother."

"Thanks, I appreciate it."

That was easier than Luc thought, though the practice of working remotely was mainstream in his industry. He could almost move to France and still keep his job. Hmm. Not an unpleasant idea. When he wasn't in such a whirlwind, he'd give that some thought too. Now he had *two* back doors available to him to get out of Texas.

Texas...what had he been thinking? Nothing wrong with the state, but oh, what he lost to get there, to get the job, which ended up being some kind of cruel mirage. He could still picture Meghan's face when she learned about his decision. She'd gone pale with shock, her eyes like dark round saucers. That was before the rage had risen to boiling. That had come quickly. Luc winced at the memory.

Why hadn't he brought it up to her first? He knew the answer to that. The job was a perfect next step for his career, and she'd only try to talk him out of it. If he were already committed to it, she'd get used to the idea and...

He shook his head. He'd been a selfish fool. No way around it. A complete idiot. His own mother, who adored and admired him—unlike his father—had almost said as much. *Put yourself in Meghan's shoes.* She'd shown a rare grimace. *Do you love her?* He hadn't been able to look his mother in the eye. *Yes*, he'd told her. His mother had stared at him for a moment, shaken her head, and left the room.

Luc sighed deeply. How often he'd endured those flashbacks. They were his penance. As if the loss of Meghan wasn't painful enough on its own.

Chapter Four

Meghan stretched and opened her eyes, scoping the unfamiliar gauzy curtains and furnishings. For an instant, she wasn't sure where she was. Nice, France. In Luc's apartment. In the same bedroom she'd occupied two years earlier. Yet Luc wasn't in the next room. For a moment, a wave of melancholy lapped around her.

"No, not going there," she muttered as she slid out of bed. It was nine-thirty, later than she usually got up, but no trace of jet lag remained. The day was hers to savor, and she would *not* get sucked into sad feelings about Luc. He surely wasn't thinking about *her*. He probably had a new Texan girlfriend by now, a lanky six-foot tall supermodel with flowing blond hair. She probably looked great in cowboy boots.

Meghan showered and chose a light pink cotton above-knee dress to wear. And since she was *not* a Texan supermodel, but a mere five foot five, she put on her favorite wedge sandals, perfect with the dress. With a crossbody bag and straw hat in place, she was ready to find breakfast.

While she dated Luc, she'd studied French and practiced occasionally with him. Admittedly, she'd

Postcard from Nice Kyle Hunter

let it go after their break-up, but in the days prior to her flight, she'd plowed into reviewing what little she remembered. At least she could order and understand things in restaurants and basic signage. According to Luc, she'd developed a decent accent and had a facility for language learning. That day, she'd put it to the test.

Not far from the apartment, she'd spied a *boulangerie* that sold a variety of fabulous-smelling breads and pastries, but also had small café tables and an espresso machine. That would be her daily breakfast ritual while she was in Nice. She did her best to order in French, then settled at a small table outside. As people passed and she took in the rhythms of the city, she savored the croissants, reveling in the buttery flakiness. And how did they make the coffee taste so delicious? Everything tasted better in France. She *did* remember that.

Meghan bought a tram pass, though she wouldn't need it that day. She loved riding in trams, like a smooth, efficient above-ground metro. Later, she'd just ride on one for the fun of it and to get an overview of the town. That day, her plan was to explore the Old Town and dally on the waterfront. In a day or so, she'd start taking train trips to the many fabulous towns within a short distance of Nice. She clearly remembered the advantage of many lovely towns within a thirty-minute train ride away. It had been easy to hop on and off and find oneself in a new stunning coastal wonderland to discover.

Before leaving Atlanta, she'd caught Shane up on the sordid details of her failure at work and the gracious response of her boss, Emily. Then, when she told Shane what she planned to do, her friend had fallen silent.

Really? You're going to France by yourself to the same town you went with Luc?

Meghan had fully expected this caring response from her friend, who'd comforted her through months of tears. *Of course. It was one of my favorite places on earth and it was the only place I really wanted to go. Having been there with Luc shouldn't ruin it for me.*

I hope you're right. A hint of glumness had laced Shane's voice. *I just don't want you to be sad while you're there.*

Meghan shook her head, a smile glued on her face. *Ah, my dear sweet Shane. I know how to not be sad in one of the prettiest towns in France. Just you wait. I'll have the time of my life. I'll keep you updated. I'll send a postcard or two.*

Oh, okay.

Shane had sounded like she wasn't buying Meghan's bravado. But she'd show her. Starting today.

Was it too early to call? Meghan took off her watch to change the time, which she'd forgotten to do. Yes, it was too early. She'd call Shane and her dad later in the day, when it was morning for them. Her dad's procedure had been Wednesday, and she'd been able to talk to him before leaving. In the meantime, she'd text Shane. Her friend would see the message when she woke up.

Just enjoyed my first French breakfast of café au lait and two croissants. Yummy. Wish you were here!

She grinned, knowing she'd make her friend just a tad bit jealous. It would have been more fun to be there together, but it wasn't meant to be. She took a last sip of coffee and leaned back to survey the awakening city street. A wave of joy coursed through her. Instead of being fired, she beheld her next adventure, the stunning city of Nice, with full permission. What a gift it was, a gift from Emily.

A gift from God. Along with contentment, Meghan felt humbled by the gift of being there. The special smile of God. Over the years, God had shown her she was special to him, despite her shock at being an *accident*. A chuckle emerged from her chest. Yes, it had been a devastating truth for a seven-year-old. But soon she understood her parents wanted and loved her and, in fact, had been thrilled to have another child.

Was there something she was supposed to ponder while she enjoyed the Riviera all alone for two weeks? To learn about herself? Surely, she had a lot to think about, like her flaws, her fears. And assorted defects that haunted her and tainted her relationships. For example, in her recent breakup with Adam, who, surprisingly, she hadn't thought much about in a couple of days. Things seemed to go well. Then suddenly, he cooled off. She'd tried to talk about it, and he'd claimed it was work, nothing to be concerned about. He said that until the end.

Were her expectations too high? Why were men always leaving her? Why had Luc left? Then Adam? Why did her own mother leave? Well, she didn't leave Meghan, but her dad. Still, did their family mean nothing? Did marriage vows mean nothing? Was it true, as her mother had claimed, that her kids were settled, and she had a right to her own happiness? As if somehow being their mother and their father's wife had made her unhappy?

Her sisters, Jenn and Mia, thought it was fine that their mother was starting over. But they had their own lives and families across the country. It didn't touch them like it did Meghan.

She had to admit, she expected too much from people. She was unsure where that came from, but knew it had sometimes caused stress in her relationships with friends as well as boyfriends.

High standards led to higher-than-average let-downs, she learned. She tried to change her expectations in order to protect her heart. And let people off the hook.

But with Luc, it had been black and white. He'd been black, plainly wrong.

Meghan groaned. There she was again, letting those old thoughts invade her first day in Nice. She'd shake them away and buy something cute in the Old Town. A sure cure.

The previous day, she'd wandered through the maze of boutiques along narrow alleys, but had given into her travel fatigue. That day, she'd return, not just to browse, but to shop. She wouldn't overdo it, though. As it was, she'd be paying off this little excursion for the next few months. Sadly, she had no one except Shane to buy gifts for. And postcards. She thought of Emily, too, for whom her gratitude still flowed.

She could get her mother something for Christmas. Her dad wouldn't be interested in handmade soaps or lavender sachets, available in abundance in sidewalk stalls and storefronts. Maybe he'd like a T-shirt.

Along with inviting shops, she passed some stunning buildings that forced her to stop and take photos. The lemony yellow Baroque masterpiece, le Musée Lascaris, the equally sunshine-toned

Chapelle du Saint-Sépulchre, and the national theatre.

Amidst the colorfully cheerful surroundings—and despite her need to keep her thoughts light—they frequently wandered back to Luc, like a magnet. They'd walked through those very cobbled alleys covered with awnings or shadowed by the tall medieval buildings on either side. It had been a magical time when nothing could touch them. It seemed that every few feet they strolled, he pulled her close and planted a kiss on her forehead or her lips.

Do you like this one? He'd held an apron emblazoned with lavender appliques against his chest, an impish arc to his brows.

She'd enjoyed the playful side of him, which had emerged slowly over time. *I think it's tacky enough even for you.*

Ha! I was thinking of this for you.

And so, the banter flowed.

Seemed he was falling a little in love with her too back then. Had she misread him? Meghan had learned of Luc's new job opportunity by accident. She'd been at his apartment and had seen a document with details about his move and start date on his desk. She'd confronted him, but not given him sufficient time to fully explain his thinking. Her fighting instinct, always at the ready, had kicked in full strength. Luc had suggested they try long distance for a while, then decide together, though he'd already accepted the job. Instead of following his idea, she'd blown up. And blown out of his life. Blocked his number. Then moved to Atlanta.

Kind of extreme, in retrospect. She'd been driven by...not rage, brokenness. Brokenness from being abandoned by the man she loved. Left behind, as if she'd meant nothing.

But what should she have done? He was taking a job over a thousand miles from where she was. How else could she interpret that? Had she gone too far?

She could have simply continued her life in Virginia without uprooting and giving him no way to contact her since then. He might have had second thoughts, might have changed his mind and realized he loved her. But she'd shut that door for good.

The bald truth ground a hole in her stomach. He'd accused her of holding a grudge till eternity. Luc had a point. Who was she to hold a grudge? If she were truthful, she might still love him. But she'd never know. Her stubborn choice to mete out consequences blocked her from ever finding out.

Why were her thoughts going to all these uncomfortable places?

She'd reached the end of the Old Town and approached the waterfront, where she'd stroll along the Avenue des Anglais, with turquoise water on one side and a row of decadently expensive hotels on the other. She was determined to shake her thought patterns. Again. What was done was done. The future awaited. God promised a wonderful future, despite her mistakes. She'd choose to believe it.

ఇ ఇ ఇ

Luc had made the trip many times, could almost navigate it blindfolded. Except that the circumstances weren't at all the same. That reminder settled a weight deeper into his chest as he waited for his suitcase to arrive on the conveyer. Second time in a month.

Over his lifetime since his family moved to the States, they'd returned to France every summer for a month to visit *Mamie* and reconnect with their French heritage. His mom loved her adopted second home as much or more than his father did. Fabrice, *Bryce*, seemed to take all the treasures of his homeland for granted.

During those summer visits, the family stayed at the Cassini apartment. Max and Luc shared a bedroom. They'd eat breakfast on the balcony then hit the beach a few minutes' walk away. Or they'd spend the day at *Mamie*'s and *Papi*'s house inland on a hillside, running around their tiny yard. They were the happiest moments of his young life. Despite the somber reason for his visit, the mental camera roll of those many summers flushed warmth and gratitude through his sleepy mind.

He deeply regretted not being able to stay at Cassini during his visit, though he wasn't surprised someone had booked it. Part of him wanted to grasp the last filaments of his remembrances of *Mamie* before she slipped away, out of his life forever. That apartment was a big piece of her memory, of his childhood and youth. Later, she and *Papi* purchased Riquier. Since it was bigger, she thought the family would be more comfortable there. But Luc always preferred Cassini, with its long balcony and sunny exposure. It was closer to town and the beach too.

Sébastian had said there was a renter there for two weeks, but no one was at Riquier. Was there any chance the renter would be willing to move for the second week? He'd ask Sébastian later, after coffee and breakfast, and a visit to his grandmother.

He scanned the traffic for Julien's car. Only a week earlier, it was Max and his silver Mustang. Luc lifted his fingers when he recognized the familiar blue Peugeot. He slung his bag into the back seat and hopped in before his friend could alight.

"How was your trip?" the man asked. Everyone's favorite question. Julien stuck out his hand and grasped Luc's. He'd known Julien his whole life. A longtime friend of *Papi*'s, Julien was over eighty now, six years younger than his *Mamie*, but still in sturdy shape, despite his thinning hair and body.

"It was fine, if you don't mind not sleeping. Actually, I did catch about an hour or so. Had a squirming kid next to me, but it was okay overall." He paused and met Julien's gaze. "How is she?"

Julien's creased face, though weathered, held sharp, observant eyes now showing compassion. "She could be hanging on for your sake until she can see you. Could be weeks, could be days. We just don't know."

"At least she's able to stay at home. I'm thankful for that." There was much more to be thankful for. That she was there in his life every moment from his birth until now. Maybe he could let her go, knowing that she'd had a good life, and he'd been a part of it. And vice versa. After *Papi*'s death, she moved into a smaller apartment in the coastal town of Beaulieu-sur-Mer, an upscale casino town with a view of the water. Luc would go there directly. He'd see her for himself, unwilling to take tomorrow for granted.

Once inside *Mamie*'s five-story building, Julien let them into her apartment. "*Tu es là, Luc!*" A scratchy, frail voice emerged from a cloud of linens on a hospital bed that dominated the living room.

Luc approached the bed, seeing the same gaze, and a muted version of her familiar smile, though everything else seemed withered. He sat on the edge of the bed and kissed her cheeks.

"*Viens ici,*" she croaked and held out both arms. He buried between them, as he'd done as a child, and let her wrap bony arms around him. "*Mon garçon, tu es là. Enfin.*"

Tears stung his eyes, but he smiled at her and responded in French. "Yes, I came. Finally." He repeated her words.

"You've just arrived?" Her gaze toggled between Luc and Julien.

"Yes, I just picked Luc up at the airport this morning."

"Have you eaten?" Typical *Mamie*, but Luc was glad she asked, just as a groan came from his stomach.

"Julien, there is a meal the aides prepared in the kitchen. Please... go get it and make coffee for us." Though her words came out slowly, softly, her request was clear.

After a breakfast of baguettes with butter, ham, and a soft-boiled egg with coffee, Luc felt less light-headed. Everything tasted better in France. "I won't stay long today, *Mamie*. I just wanted to see you."

"Thank you...for coming, Luc. I know you have a...busy life in the States." She spoke in measured cadence, as if speaking at all was too great an effort. Still, a cheeky smile slid through. "Do you have a girlfriend?"

Her question took him off guard. But once a grandmother, always one. That was her question of choice. "What happened to that...nice girl you brought here to Nice? Are you...still with her? I remember her." Her words emerged in labored gasps.

The reference was a knife in Luc's gut, a reminder of his failings with Meghan. "Um, we broke up, back when I moved to Texas."

She tsked a few times and shook her head. "Should...not have let her...go. Perfect for you."

He exchanged glances with Julien, who hid a grin. "I'll meet someone else one day. I'm too busy at work."

She shook her head again, disapproval etched clearly on her face. "Luc, work is just work. Love is... more important...than work. Don't work until it's too late...and you are alone." Another slice from the knife. How right she was. It was hitting home, but too late, as her words predicted.

"We should let you rest, Isabelle." Julien rose. "Luc can come back again."

"Wait." She held up her hand and looked at Luc. "I need a favor. I need something...can you find...

from Cassini. A diary. I want to see it. Haven't seen it in years...in the *placard*."

But the Cassini apartment was rented for another week and a half. How would he pull this off? "I'll find a way, *Mamie*. I'll get it. What does it look like?"

"It's small. Flowered. Has...memories. I need to see it before I leave. I lost the key... You'll break the lock for me."

Luc smiled and grasped her hand. "I'll do my best." He stooped forward and kissed her temple. "I'll see you soon."

When they returned to Julien's car, he asked Luc, "Where to? Cassini?"

"Unfortunately, Cassini is booked for the next week and a half. I'll be staying at Riquier, but need to get the key from Sébastian. You know the Pierrot Agency?"

"*Oui*, I know it. If someone's staying at Cassini, how will you get the diary your grandmother wants?"

"I'm going to try to sweet-talk the renter into spending the second week of their reservation at Riquier at a discount. I'll have access to the owner's cupboard, but also, I want to...just spend some time there. It'll do me good."

"Yes, it will. You spent lots of time there every summer. I hope you can stay there during your visit."

Luc had never tried something like this with an established renter. To offer a larger apartment at the same price as the small one should be a no-brainer for most budget-conscious tourists. Only it was farther from the waterfront and Old Town.

If it didn't work, he'd just tell them he needed to access the cupboard, and it should be fine. *If* he could find the diary. The next time he spoke to his grandmother, he'd ask for more details about what to look for, what kind of box the diary was in... but she was almost ninety. How long had it been since she'd seen the diary? And why did she want it now? Well, that was her business, but his chances of getting any more information from her were slim.

He arrived at the Pierrot agency and went inside while Julien waited in the car, double parked. He nodded at Sébastian's receptionist when he entered. "Séb is here? He's expecting me. I'm Luc Badaux."

"Yes, I'll tell him you're here, Monsieur Badaux."

An office door opened. "Luc, welcome back. I have a key for you. Come, come." The older man shook Luc's hand, and he slid into a chair facing a large desk. Fatigue from the flight was starting to hit him, but he had to do a couple more things before he could collapse on the bed.

Sébastian slid a key across the desk. "Here's the key to the Riquier apartment. It's yours for the next two weeks, or however long you want to stay. That said, it's got a reservation first of next month."

"I'll be long gone by then. I have a request. I would prefer to stay in Cassini for my visit, not only for personal reasons. I need something from the storage closet there. How about offering the renters or renter—"

"It's a single female," supplied Sébastian.

"How about asking her to move to Riquier for her second week at the same price as Cassini?"

Sébastian's eyebrows lifted. "I can try. I'll explain the owner needs access. We'll see what she says. The Riquier is an attractive property and bigger. I can try to sell her on this, like a free upgrade."

"Thanks. That ought to work." He rose and took the key. "Keep me posted."

"I won't promise anything. It's a bit, uh, unorthodox, but you're the owner."

Chapter Five

Meghan treasured her memories of Antibes, the smaller jewel on the coast, a town to the west of Nice, where she and Luc had gone. They'd spent a day there, strolling atop the ramparts surrounding the town, wandering along the edge of the marina where the yachts lined up like long, elegant swans. Then they ate lunch at one of the cafés along the wall of arches that separated the town from the piers.

That day, as the local train carried her toward Antibes, she braced herself for more memories. Overall, she hadn't done that badly with stale recollections of her days with Luc. He appeared in her thoughts, in her mind's eye too frequently—understandably. But the initial ache those images brought lessened each day. Funny how she thought about him more often than she did Adam.

If she'd been able to bring a traveling companion with her, thoughts of Luc would have remained at bay. But alone with her own company, keeping her mind disciplined was a challenge. She persisted and knew that with practice, it was possible.

Postcard from Nice *Kyle Hunter*

Toward the end of a satisfying day meandering under the sunshine, she settled onto a bench near a large square with jets of water shooting upward at different heights. Several small children dashed between them, trying not to get wet, shrieking with laughter as they ran the gauntlet. In the end, most of them were soaked, but the warmth of the day made it a pleasurable game.

She glanced at her watch. It was a good time to call Dad. She tapped his number and after a few rings, heard the voice of her father's wife, Jill.

"Hi, Jill. It's Meghan. Just wanted to check in on Dad. Is he awake?"

"Hey, Meghan. Good to hear from you. Yes, he's here and wants to talk to you too. He got home from the hospital Saturday. Here he is."

"Hi, Dad," Meghan said once her father was on the phone. "How are you feeling?"

"I won't run any races yet, but they say it'll just take a couple weeks."

"Before you can run a race?" Meghan chuckled. "I'm glad everything went well."

"Like clockwork. They have these robots that do the surgery. Well, there are two surgeons that operate the robots. Not sure how to explain it, but it makes the whole process faster with quicker recovery. That's what they told me, in any case. I'll let you know if it's true."

"It's amazing what they can do. I guess that's called AI heart surgery."

Her father laughed. "You could say that. Are you in France, Meggie?"

"I got here Saturday, the same day you got home from the hospital."

They talked a few more minutes about Meghan's trip and her father's expected recovery. "I don't want to tire you out, Dad."

"No worries. I'm glad you got to France safely. Does your mother know you're there?"

Guilt poked at Meghan. Though her parents were no longer married, her father often encouraged Meghan to overcome her negative feelings about the divorce. "Um, not yet. It all happened so fast."

She heard him sigh. "Okay, if you say so. It's a big event, going to France. I'm sure she'd like to know about it."

"Yeah. You're right."

"Meggie, I hope you'll one day put your mother's decisions behind you. We all have, and you need to as well." His words struck her like a hammer. It was true. Why hadn't she let go of the hurt? The *disapproval*? Who was *she* to disapprove?

"You're right, Dad. I'll get in touch with her today. I'll send her an email."

"Good. Think about what I said."

"I will, Dad." They hung up and his words rang inside. While the phone sat warm in her hand, she jotted an email to her mother, briefly explaining why she was in France. Put it behind her. Everyone but Meghan had done that. Nothing would be gained by her hanging on, keeping a grudge. Luc's words added an echo to the twist of conviction. He once said she could hold a grudge for eternity. Was that true?

Meghan decided to stay in for dinner that evening. Since she had an apartment with a full kitchen, there was no use spending money daily on restaurants. Besides, she didn't relish eating alone around other people who were *not*. Eating at home alone was different. She'd bought a large bag of groceries the day before. That removed the excuse that she had nothing in the fridge.

And she was tired. Four days in Nice and she hadn't sat still very long. Tomorrow she'd go to Villefranche, an enchanting coastal town that was close by. After that, either the hilltop village of Eze or Menton, the sunny citrus capital along the Italian border. So many choices and all of them were good. That night she'd make a salad, broil some salmon, and read a novel.

Once she'd changed into jogging shorts and a tank, she started dinner. She and Luc had cooked at home several times during their stay. Those evenings were almost more special to her than going to a restaurant. It had felt like being at home, like a married couple, working together in the kitchen and enjoying it on the balcony under a mauve sunset as the balmy breeze caressed the busy day to its close. Then curling up together on the couch, talking late into the night...

"Stop that." Meghan's voice rang aloud through the apartment. "Stop thinking of the past. Of Luc. He's history. This is his place, but he's not here. Get over it."

She redoubled her effort on thinking of the meal. Seasoning the salmon. Preparing the salad. Opening the wine. (Yes, she'd bought a bottle of Provence rosé to enjoy all alone.)

Her cell phone rang. Who could be calling her in France? Her mother, responding to her email? Someone in the States who didn't realize she was in Europe. She looked at her phone. Pierrot Agency? What did they want?

"Allô?" She'd get as far as the basic greeting, but would have to continue in English.

"Mademoiselle Clark, this is Sébastian from the rental agency. I trust you are enjoying your stay in Nice."

"Yes, it's been lovely. It's one of my favorite cities in the world." It was true. She'd fallen in love with both Luc and Nice, and was still in love with Nice.

"I have a proposition to suggest to you that you may find appealing."

The smooth, salesy tone of his voice caused warning bells to ring in her imagination. What proposition?

"What is that?"

"The owner of your apartment had to make an emergency visit to Nice, and he would be very appreciative if you would consider moving to a different apartment for your second week. It's a more spacious apartment, more elegant than the one you are in, and he would charge you the same amount, no more. Consider it an upgrade at no extra cost."

Beads of perspiration popped out on Meghan's neck and forehead. *Luc was in Nice?* She came all the way to Nice and Luc Badaux was *there?*

She lowered onto the couch, her knees unsteady. Did he know she was there? No, it wasn't likely. But it was possible, since Luc was the owner. He'd have the right to see rental records. She didn't know how to ask that question to Sébastian without announcing that she knew Luc.

But the other point was...how dare he! She'd paid good money to reserve this specific apartment on this street and he had no right to ask her to move, even to a larger apartment. "No, I'm afraid not, Sébastian, but thanks for the offer. I'm quite comfortable here. I've found my landmarks for groceries, the tram, things like that. I'd like to stay here."

"Even for an upgrade to a larger apartment at the same rate?"

"What would I need with a larger apartment? I'm one person and I'm very happy where I am. I'm sure the owner will understand that once a unit is rented, it belongs to the tenant for that period. It's a legal agreement, you see." She kept her voice calm, though her heart pounded against her ribs. Luc was there. Luc was in Nice.

"I understand. It's unusual that I would even make this request. But when he arrived unexpectedly—his grandmother is dying—he made this request."

Oh. Meghan's spirits dropped. She'd met Luc's grandmother once and had liked her, finding the woman wise and observant. She didn't pull any punches for anyone. Her blunt remarks had spurred Meghan to laughter several times during their brief acquaintance.

And she was dying. "I'm sorry about the owner's grandmother." She almost slipped and said *Luc's grandmother*. "Sincerely, I am. But I rented this apartment in good faith for an agreed-upon period of time."

"Yes, you're right, you did. You're not interested in a larger apartment at the same price?"

"No, I'm afraid not. If there's another apartment available, perhaps the owner can stay there?"

"Yes, he most likely will. If you're sure..." Sébastian's voice trailed off.

Meghan was relieved he wasn't going to strong-arm her into agreeing. Even if Luc wasn't the one making the request, she had no desire to leave Cassini. She loved that place. Luc did too, she knew. Not surprising that he'd want to stay there during his visit. It was a treasured place, he'd told her, full of sparkling memories of childhood. Those days of innocence, before life got harder, more confusing. One evening as candlelight flickered from a candle on the coffee table, Luc told her tales of his boyhood in Nice, all the summers he and Max had spent there. Sounded magical. No wonder he preferred Cassini to the other place. She faltered, caught up in Luc's nostalgia.

Well, too bad, Badaux.

"Yes, I'm quite sure," she said as she realized Sébastian awaited confirmation of her refusal.

"I'll let him know."

After disconnecting, she bit her lip. Was she doing the right thing?

Meghan fluttered nervously in the kitchen, finishing her meal preparation. All the while, her thoughts ran races around her skull. She'd been in Nice four days and had thought about Luc at least eight hundred times since her arrival. Had she summoned his presence by her thoughts? She mocked the idea, though a bolt of anxiety cut into the sound, turning it to a whimper. At least she hadn't agreed to his request, which was unreasonable. Even with his grandmother dying, unless that was a lie meant to soften her up. No, Isabelle had been ancient even two years earlier when Meghan had met her. It was likely true that she was in her final days.

The question was, did Meghan want to see Luc? She didn't know. She was still hurt by what he'd done. Yet, since her arrival, he'd been in her thoughts, and she admitted to herself she might still love him. And here he was.

But what about him? He was the one who had walked out on *her*. It didn't matter if she loved him or not, or might be open to loving him again.

It was irrelevant, because *he* had left *her*.

ೆ ೆ ೆ

Luc crossed his arms over his chest and one ankle over his other knee, irritation trickling through him. She'd refused. Disappointing and frustrating, but if he were being fair, he'd have done the same.

"I tried, Luc." Sébastian's tone was mild. "She was polite, but said what we both know. She entered into a contract to rent this unit, and it's technically hers until the end of her agreed-upon lease."

"I know, I know. Lots of people would have accepted the deal and so, well, she's not one of them." He felt like a petulant boy. The renter's attitude wouldn't block him from accessing the owner's closet and searching for his grandmother's diary. It might be a chance to go in there himself and see what he still had there.

A fresh idea sailed into his mind. He'd try that, then give up. "One more thought." He tapped the edge of Sébastian's desk. "Why don't you make the same offer, but knock off two days from the rent for the second week?"

Sébastian's bushy eyebrows lifted. "Two days? You want this so badly?"

"Since I'm here, I'd like to stay in Cassini."

"You could have come and stayed there any time in the last couple of years. I know you're here because of your grandmother, but it's not a pleasure visit. It's a sad occasion."

"All the more reason to find refuge in Cassini." He met Sébastian's gaze, knowing he was taking this thing too far. Something inside him needed it. Reconnection, just as he was watched his French root system crumble beneath him. The footings of his childhood. "So, try. After that, I'll give up. But I'll still need to access the closet."

"Understood." Sébastian sighed. "I'll reach out to the renter again and see what she says."

"Thanks."

Later that day, Luc waited on the platform for the train to Villefranche. Julien was picking him up at the station so they could return to visit *Mamie*. He'd texted his mom to give her a status report after seeing his grandmother.

It was good to be back on the Cote d'Azur, despite the circumstances. Even the air smelled different. While he waited, his gaze wandered among the clusters of people waiting farther down on the platform. For an instant, he saw a woman resembling Meghan. The same clothing style, haircut, height. His eyes narrowed to get a better look, then she vanished behind a pole. Meghan invaded his thoughts, even in France.

His phone rang with a US number. From Chicago.

"Hi Luc, this is Freddie Harmon. I know you're still in France, but I took the liberty of calling you to let you know I received your resume the other day by email. I was very impressed. So far, it appears you'd fit well into the position I'm creating."

"Thanks, Freddie. I appreciate that. I'm glad you received the resume."

"I don't plan to keep you long on the phone, but wondered about your level of interest. If you're leaning toward other options, I'll pursue someone else who's second on my list."

"I'm very interested, given what I know about the position. Can you send me a detailed job description?"

"I'm traveling as well, but will get that to you as soon as I can."

"Is it a remote position?"

"Not necessarily. I prefer on site, at least part-time. But if that's important to you, I'd be open to talking about it after a few months of training and connecting with the team at the office."

They chatted a few more minutes about the position, then disconnected. The man had a warm, friendly tone, which hopefully meant he'd be easy to work with, flexible and relaxed. One never knew.

When Luc and Julien arrived in Beaulieu, Luc's grandmother was sleeping. Once she stirred and recognized them, a gentle smile stretched across her face. "I'm glad… you're here."

"I'm more myself today, *Mamie*. Yesterday I was very tired after the flight."

"*Oui…c'est normal.*"

She'd changed significantly in the last year, when he and Max had made a brief visit on the way to Italy for a vacation. That time, they'd gotten a hotel room, since Cassini had been rented. *Mamie* had just signed over Riquier to them and it wasn't ready for guests. Her eyes had been brighter, and she wasn't bedridden then. She'd moved slowly with a walker and stayed home most of the time. But after a fall last winter and a bout of pneumonia, her health spiraled downward.

With a slight gesture of her head toward Julien, he stood. "I'm on it." He strode into the kitchen and returned with a plate of store-bought cookies, cheese, and fruit.

"I hope you were hungry," he murmured to Luc.

"I'm sure you didn't...have time to... the diary?" *Mamie* whispered.

"No, not yet." Luc took her cool, crepey hand in his. "Someone is renting the apartment, so I will make arrangements to drop by. Is there anything else you want from the closet while I'm over there?"

"I...wouldn't remember it." She made an effort at smiling again. It made Luc want to cry.

"That's probably true. How should I recognize the diary? Is it this big?" He measured a space with his hands about six inches long. "Or this big?" He stretched his arms out wide until she emitted a weak chuckle. "It's full of secrets? You'd need one that big, *Mamie*. You'd need a few volumes for all your secrets and misdeeds, right?"

"*Oui. C'est ça.*" She gestured with her fingers. The journal must be only about eight inches long.

"Flowered?"

She nodded.

They didn't stay long, seeing that Isabelle had grown sleepy. That suited Luc, since he didn't want his visit to wear her out. She seemed happy enough to receive the two of them for a short time.

While Julien drove him back to Nice, Luc phoned Sébastien.

"I wish I had better news for you, Luc, but she refused again. She said again, it was a kind offer, but she liked where she was. I think we should leave this alone for now."

"Fine. Okay, how do I go about getting into the closet? I need something for my grandmother. You can give me a key and I'll go over there, ring the bell, and if she doesn't answer, I can assume she's out for the day."

"You'd have to notify her of access."

"Can you let her know for me? Say the owner needs to access the locked cupboard but doesn't want to disturb her. I can give a window of when I'll be there or else just say sometime tomorrow. She'll have no interest in meeting the owner. That'll give me some time to go through the closet while she's off on an excursion."

"Sounds like a better plan. You let me know when you'll be there, and I'll notify her."

Luc sighed. He hoped he could find it the first time. This renter was turning into a royal pain.

Chapter Six

Meghan didn't sleep well that night, despite her fatigue and more than one glass of rosé. Her mind chugged like a train over the same question. Did she want to see Luc?

Under the weird current circumstances, it might not be difficult to have a *chance* meeting with him if she wanted that. And she wasn't sure she did. Her mind played out several scenarios during the night. She could ask Sébastian to let Luc know the identity of the renter and ask if he wanted to speak with her himself. That was the direct approach. It didn't guarantee an encounter, because he could choose not to see her. That would hurt. But it was one option.

It would open more pain and require more recovery. Maybe that wasn't such a great idea. It had been a year and a half. True, he'd tried to reach out to her after the fact, probably with a belated realization of what an unfeeling egoist he'd been. But over time, he'd surely moved on. What if he was married? What if his wife came with him to Nice?

A cold flush rippled down her skin at the thought. That would be humiliating. But at least she'd stop wondering if she'd made the biggest mistake of her life to turn away from him.

Following breakfast and coffee on the balcony—which she'd discovered was as appealing or more so than eating at the boulangerie—she paced the living room. And thought. And paced and thought. What other scenario would be more natural than contacting the Pierrot office? Just as she considered that question, Sébastian had phoned her again and increased his offer to two nights free if she would accept. She did not. That principle was still in force.

She could always contact Sébastian and ask for a phone call directly from the owner, saying she was considering his offer after all. Which she wasn't. But it would put her in contact with Luc. But her ruse to get him to call might annoy him. Scratch that.

Meghan forced herself out the door right after lunch, having wound herself up in a knot. This new situation could easily derail the blissful path of her Nice vacation, if she allowed it. She would not.

Instead, she bought a train ticket to Menton, just beyond Monaco. She'd visited once before. With Luc. This time, she'd make her *own* memories. The train climbed higher and higher along rocky cliffs, giving a stunning view of azure waters glistening far below, hemming elegant homes along the carved coastline.

She might be taking a chance on missing Luc altogether, since she didn't know how long he was staying. It was too easy to try to figure everything out, all the angles, by herself. She knew better. She knew because she'd learned it the hard way. Doing things by herself—like the scrappy, self-protective child she knew she still resembled—was exhausting. Jesus had said his yoke was *easy*, his burden was *light*. Yet her knee-jerk reaction was to pull all the burden onto her own shoulders. *Lord, I'm going to give this to you. I don't know what to do, whether I should see Luc or not. Or try to. I hope you'll show me clearly what to do, because I have no idea.*

The hilly town of Menton extended its invitation, with cinnamon orange and ochre buildings and towering palms along the waterfront, in some ways, similar to Villefranche. She was glad she'd chosen to come, to rid her mind of the decision that weighed on her. And she adored the town.

Every few minutes, though, her thoughts wandered back. Would it be emotionally difficult to see him again, after such a long time, following the fight that ended their romance? Maybe he'd forgotten about that, about her. *Meghan who? Oh, yeah. She was jealous of my career. I dodged a bullet.* Regret pinched her inside. It wasn't the fact he took a job in another state, but the *way* he did it, without discussing it. She frowned. *And* the fact that he did it.

Her phone vibrated in her purse. Sébastian again! What could he want this time?

"Hello, Miss Clark. I apologize for calling you so many times. The owner has accepted your decision and will not trouble you further. There is just one thing."

"What is that?" Her spirits sagged when she heard Luc wouldn't trouble her further.

"In the apartment, there is a locked closet where the owner stores personal items. He needs to access this area at some point, tomorrow or the next day. If you don't mind, he can come in while you're on an excursion, so you won't be disturbed. He'll get what he needs from the closet and leave. Of course, he won't disturb any of your items while he's there."

Meghan took a breath. "That sounds fine. Will he notify me when he is coming?"

"I will do this myself once I know his plans, to offer the least disturbance possible to you."

She bit her lip. Luc would not be making the call himself. That would have made it easy to at least speak with him, feel him out in advance. "I don't mind if he calls me himself." She paused. "How long will he be in Nice?"

"I believe at least a week, but depending on his grandmother's situation...He doesn't know for sure."

"I'm sure it's a very difficult time for him." She softened her voice. It was a hard time for Luc. She should try to be sympathetic. Or at least sound like she was. "I'm sorry I wasn't able to accommodate his request."

"You are very kind. It is not your problem. You are on vacation, so he should not have made the request."

True. "It's no problem. It would be good to know which day he'll come."

"Yes, that's understandable. Tomorrow or the following day. I will ask him his plans."

"Right. Depending on his grandmother."

"Yes, you understand."

She did. There would be no easy way to see Luc, even if she was sure she wanted to. Which a big part of her, she had to admit, did.

ଔ ଔ ଔ

Luc had planned to go to the apartment tomorrow or the next day. He'd had every intention of complying with the requirement to let the renter know he was coming. But when he found himself on Rue Cassini staring up like a beggar at his former summer home, he decided to take a chance. He approached the row of buttons by the front door and rang at the one marked *Badaux*. There was no response, so he took the liberty of buzzing himself in and riding to the fifth floor.

The apartment looked the same, just somehow more...feminine. A novel lay face-down on the coffee table, and by the door sat a pair of chunky heeled shoes, the kind Meghan used to wear. At the thought, a pang hit him.

Luc went to the locked closet and opened it. Stacks of plastic boxes greeted him. He groaned. How long would this take? He'd better get started. If memory served him, there were only a few boxes in one corner containing his grandmother's things, and the rest belonged to him. When she downsized, she'd gotten rid of most of the excess. What was the story with the diary?

While he worked opening boxes, leafing through them and simultaneously watching over one shoulder, his thoughts floated back to Meghan. He'd noticed her at the office shortly after she started working there. He thought...wow. Adorable and sexy all at once. She usually wore short dresses, some kind of heels, and coordinating jewelry. Her dark, straight hair came down past her chin, then curled under. The total effect was feminine-corporate. To the extreme. It drew him, as did her perky teasing, though he'd pretended to be annoyed.

Only after they were dating did he understand some of her insecurities, the kind that never showed through her immaculate appearance. Or they could be the reason for it. And then, she could sometimes be pushy, though in a sweet feminine way. And anxious. He wasn't sure where that came from. Probably something from her childhood. But she claimed she was working on it. She had an endearing tendency to fight for the underdog. One of his favorite stories she'd told was from her elementary school days, when she stood up for a kid being bullied and ended up in a fight herself. She said she related to underdogs. She was a fighter, alright, and sometimes took it too far. But she had a tender side as well.

He loved the times she wore sweats and looked fully relaxed, instead of all put-together. Like after a day at the beach, when she didn't style her hair. The resulting waves made him want to run his fingers through the silky strands for a long time. He could almost smell the floral cocktail that was released when he did that...right before easing her against the cushion to kiss her.

Luc sighed as old longings stirred. It was normal to recall things about Meghan, since he was standing in the very place he'd shared with her during the most idyllic week of his adult life. Recalling things...like the perfume she wore, flowery with a hint of citrus. Her color choices, bold tones and tiny print patterns, always spot-on, though he was no expert on color or styles. He just knew she pulled it together perfectly.

Her habit of biting her lower lip if she was anxious, like when they watched a scary or tense movie together. He'd pull her closer into his chest, as if to allay any fears, even imaginary ones, she might have. To protect her. *Forever...*

"You're getting sappy, Badaux." His grumble filled the tiny room. "And you found exactly nothing. Time to scoot." He'd get a drink first. Carefully. The water cooled his dry throat, so he had another glass. Then he placed it in the dishwasher next to a few more.

Luc had opened all his grandmother's boxes in the locked cupboard and no diary. Admittedly, he hadn't removed *all* their contents. He'd mostly glanced across the surface and leafed through whatever was on top. His grandmother was close to ninety. She'd probably forgotten where she put it. Now he was impatient and sweaty in only twenty minutes. He'd wanted to finish and be gone before the renter appeared, since he hadn't warned her.

Discouraged, he let himself out of the apartment. Hopefully, his grandmother would appreciate the fact that he'd tried. He'd let her know, and would be off the hook, since it likely wasn't even there. At least he got a glimpse of Cassini while he was in town. Better than nothing.

ଔ ଔ ଔ

By the time Meghan unlocked the door that afternoon, her head pounded. She'd been doing too much running around during her so-called restful vacation. Sure didn't help that she'd slept so little the previous two nights.

She'd thoroughly enjoyed her day's excursion, Eze Village. Eze was a stunning village on a hillside topped with gardens that drew people far and wide. There was a huge variety of unusual plants she'd never seen before, and a spectacular view, as the cliffside plunged to meet the turquoise Mediterranean. She could have stared at it for hours. She hadn't wanted to leave that early, but the shooting pains began in the late afternoon. It had been at least a year since her last migraine. Not a good time or place to start again.

She needed to rest and stay in Nice the next day. Meghan had never been one who could move at warp speed day after day, on vacation or otherwise, and forego down time. She'd learn the lesson in time to salvage the rest of her stay, which was passing too fast.

Once in the apartment, Meghan kicked off her shoes and fell onto the couch, savoring the total release of her limbs, the silence of the room, though with muted city sounds floating through the closed windows. After a few minutes, she pulled herself up. No message from Sébastian that day, which was a relief. No message, no tension. No Luc. Not yet.

After a tall glass of cold water and a couple of Tylenol, the headache began to ease. She opened the French doors at the patio and let the breeze tumble into the room, chasing out the stuffy air. Even better.

Then she stilled. The dishwasher was slightly ajar. Just slightly, but still. She slid the door open, and a glass sat on the top rack. It sat among others she'd used, but it wasn't there before. *He'd been there.*

Her gaze panned the room. Everything looked as she'd left it. She padded to the owner's closet, which sat directly behind the cubby for cleaning supplies. She jiggled the doorknob. Locked, as expected. She couldn't detect anything else showing Luc's passage. Except that she felt him. Sensed him. He'd been there.

Meghan returned to the couch as her stomach clenched. He'd come, and she missed him. No one had notified her. Sébastian must have forgotten. What had she planned to do? Intercept him? She hadn't decided, really. Part of her longed to see him, and another part wanted to continue enjoying her vacation and forget once again about Luc Badaux. She'd gotten used to her life without him. Only being in Nice had stirred everything up so she *thought* she wanted to see him. Maybe she didn't.

"Reminder to self, Meghan Clark," she said aloud, listening as the sharp sound of her voice cut through the silence. "Luc Badaux abandoned you in favor of a new career in Texas." She swallowed a lump that had formed. "Without even asking what you thought in advance after one year of seriously dating. Don't. Forget. That."

Suddenly, she pictured herself running after him, abasing herself when *he'd* been the one to leave. The one to walk away from her. The ache still simmered under her skin. No, he didn't deserve a second chance.

Chapter Seven

Luc's worn sandals flopped along the sidewalk of Boulevard Riquier, nearly dry after an overnight shower. The temperature hovered in the mid-seventies, which he considered perfect. Towering plane trees cast dappled shade. It was *all* perfect. Except for the task at hand. That task annoyed him.

When he'd visited his grandmother the previous day following his stealth efforts at Cassini, he might have expected she'd insist that he hadn't looked in the right places to find the diary. Which was exactly what she did. He'd hoped she'd be grateful for his effort and realize it wasn't there. But no.

Instead, she'd given him an indulgent smile and grasped his hand. "I know it's there, Luc. I can...visualize the box. It has a purple...handle on it. It's opaque, so you might... might not have seen it inside." Through her wheezing breath he understood perfectly her iron determination.

"You could have explained the purple handle when I was here before, *Mamie*. I spent time yesterday trespassing the property while the renter was gone. I was afraid she'd come and think I was a thief or something." He paused for effect. "She might have even shot me."

His grandmother had merely puffed out a silent laugh and patted his hand. "That only happens...in America..."

He let her dismissal slide. "*Mamie*, is it possible that you've forgotten where it is? You *are*..." he stopped himself, but it had to be said.

"I'm old. Is that what...you want to say?"

He laughed. "I was going to say you're almost ninety. If the diary has been missing for even ten years, you might have forgotten where you put it."

She shook her head before he finished speaking. "Luc, my boy, it won't take long and will mean a lot to me. I'm soon to leave... this earth and I need to... see it."

"For personal reasons, I assume," Luc had muttered, hoping she'd divulge those reasons. Not that it would make a difference. He couldn't refuse her request.

Isabelle smiled, though her eyes were nearly shut. "Thank you, Luc." She murmured and turned her head on the pillow as if to dismiss him.

So, there he was. Returning to Cassini. Breaking in again, sort of. This time, he'd asked Sebastien to text the renter, so he'd covered himself. He should have told his grandmother it was the last time he'd go. But then, he wasn't in Nice on a pleasure visit, a tourist trip. He was there for her. And if that's what she wanted him to do, he'd do it. *So, stop being a grump, Badaux.*

He'd taken the morning to enjoy a leisurely breakfast on the balcony, after scoping out a boulangerie and heading home with a warm, crispy baguette. The day after his arrival, he'd stocked the fridge with a few essentials: butter for baguettes (which, according to French habit, he'd only use at breakfast), a jar of jam, yogurt, and coffee. He didn't know for sure how long he'd be in Nice.

After breakfast, he'd strolled along the streets, remembering, absorbing the place, feeling at home, despite a long absence. It was *his* town. He'd always felt completely comfortable there, like a fish in its own fishbowl. He'd adapted well to the States too, but it had never been quite the same. An adopted homeland instead of a born one. A big difference, even though he was half American.

At the end of Boulevard Riquier, he passed the rectangular Port Lympia marina. The water glinted from a cloudless sunny sky and reflected off the many speed boats parked there. Then he was on Rue Cassini. He'd make it quick. *Please, Lord. Let me find the diary...quickly.*

As he'd done the day before, he rang the apartment bell and waited. No response. It was fair game. Like a cat burglar, he let himself into the apartment, still and quiet as he'd done the day before. The shoes that had been by the door were gone, but near the couch lay a pair of pink canvas sneakers. A bottle of Tylenol sat on the coffee table.

He crept to the closet to complete his task, trying to remember which boxes he'd handled the day before. He scanned the small space for a purple handle but didn't see one. No surprise there.

For the next fifteen minutes, he looked for the purple handle, but also opened other boxes, trying to remember which ones were hers without opening everything. No luck. There wouldn't be any use in looking in the same ones. Finally, he sat back on his heels and let out a long sigh. "Sorry, *Mamie*..." The only other thing he could do was to take everything from the closet and empty each box, one at a time. He didn't relish the thought of doing that, and might wait until the renter had returned to wherever she came from.

He'd failed again. Carefully and quietly, Luc re-locked the closet door, even though he knew no one was home. Resisting the urge to get another glass of water, he strode to the balcony. His longing to sit there for just a moment stirred...oh, to enjoy the breeze and flood of past mental photos that would slip through his mind's eye. If he couldn't stay there, could he spend a mere five or ten minutes gazing out at the view he'd savored as a child and teen, hearing the sounds he'd grown up with?

Luc gingerly opened one of the French doors and propped it with a rubber floor wedge so it wouldn't slam with a sudden breeze. The dreaded *courant d'air*, which *Mamie* had always warned him about. Just ten minutes. He slipped into the chair and stared out across the city, taking in the citrus-colored buildings, wrought iron balconies, palm and acacia trees. Pink floral fans from mimosa trees...

Back home, he'd been working too hard. He should come back here for a real vacation. Maybe that's what would make the emptiness inside him disappear.

ଔ ଔ ଔ

Meghan tried to open her eyes, still weighted shut by the dream and the sense of being wrapped in a cocoon. A quiet escape to another land...where was it? She took a breath and forced her eyes open. She was in the bedroom during the day, enjoying a deep nap. Wonderful. How she'd needed it.

The first thing she noticed was the migraine was gone. "Oh, thank you, Lord." She didn't move. No need. Filtered afternoon light spilled through the shades into the womb of comfort. She pulled the sheet closer and closed her eyes. No, she wouldn't sleep again, but it was *so* comfortable lying there.

As she lay still, listening to her own breath, she heard a sound in the next room. A small one. It was an older building, and might make noises. Another noise. She tensed. Sounded like someone was in the apartment.

A prowler? Her eyes shot open. *Luc?* Was it Luc? He could have remembered something else he needed and had returned. Again, without phoning first. Her heart thumped against her ribs. If it was Luc, was she ready to see him?

She should pull herself together before he left. That is, if she *did* want to see him. Which she might, but still wasn't sure. With great effort, she slipped from the bed and checked herself in the mirror to assess the damage. She looked sleepy, but there were no pillow marks on her face. Her hair was mussed, but she was fully clothed in knit shorts and a T-shirt. She'd likely catch Luc in the process of going through the closet.

Meghan eased the bedroom door open and shot a glance across the living room. Nothing stirred. She crept out and surveyed the closet. It too was closed, locked. He must have already left. Then her gaze roved to the balcony, where one French door stood ajar. And just beyond it, she saw a man sitting in a chair as if he lived there. As if it were *his* apartment.

Maybe it *was* his apartment.

Quietly, she approached the door and stilled, looking at his back, where her hands had strayed so many times, stroking his shoulders as he held her close. Catching her breath, rebuking her heart. It was Luc, no doubt about it. Wavy light brown hair still curled below his ears. She couldn't tell anything else about him from that angle. And she couldn't determine how she felt, standing there about to see Luc Badaux for the first time in ages.

"What are you doing here?" she asked.

Luc flinched and craned his head toward her voice. When he saw her, his mouth dropped open, and he stood, almost knocking the chair over. "Meghan?" His voice spiked with surprise.

They stood still for a split second, staring at each other. He looked the same, with the familiar long lines down his jaws, green-hazel eyes looking astonished and confused. Though Meghan wasn't surprised, she still wanted to pinch herself to believe what she was seeing.

"What are *you* doing here?" His voice emerged without warmth, a trace of accusation lacing the edges.

His tone made her bristle. "I happen to be renting the apartment, which you likely already know."

"I didn't know it was you."

"And if you had?" she challenged.

"I...I don't know." He rubbed one hand over his chin. "I'm surprised. I don't know what to say."

"Hello? How about that, for starters?" She crossed her arms.

"Why'd you come *here*? To Nice?"

She blinked. Is that all he had to say? "I *like* it here. I was overdue for vacation, and I thought, where do I want to go? This is what came to mind."

"Why the same apartment?"

"Why not? It's familiar. It's central." As a paying renter, she did not have to justify herself.

Silence dripped between them.

"Look," she said. "My money is as good as anyone else's. I rented this place fair and square. It's right on my credit card."

"And you're the one who didn't want to leave." A tiny grin emerged on one side of his memorably sensuous mouth. "Feisty Meghan. I remember that."

She didn't answer. "Why did *you* come back? To the apartment?"

"You knew I was here yesterday?"

"Yes. I thought Sébastian was going to phone me. I know it's your apartment, but I entered a contract and have the right—"

Luc held up a hand. "I apologize for entering—twice—without letting you know. I did ask Séb to text you about today." He blew out a puff of air and his posture drooped.

"I didn't see it. I had a headache and took a nap."

"I didn't find what I was looking for yesterday, so I had to come back today. It's...it's something for my grandmother. She asked me to find something for her. I'd never have come here for anything less. Anything for me. I don't know why it's so important for her, but..." he shrugged. "She's dying."

Meghan relaxed her shoulders. "I'm sorry about your grandmother. I liked her." She almost grinned at the memory of the salty older woman the one time she'd met her, but it seemed inappropriate in view of Luc's statement.

"Thanks." His eyes cut away from hers. "She's ready, she says. She wants to see the Lord."

"I'm glad she feels that way. I remember she influenced your faith."

Luc's expression softened, and he offered a small smile. "I wouldn't have any faith if it weren't for her. Though it's been struggling lately."

She blinked and moistened her lips. "Join the club."

"Should we sit?" Luc gestured to the other chair. "Or we can stand until we decide how this awkward meeting will turn out."

Keeping her gaze on his, Meghan lowered herself in the chair. Her heartbeat had slowed slightly, but was still annoyingly vigorous. "So, you tried to boot me from the apartment so you could look for the thing your grandmother wanted?"

"Basically, yes. But I...I wanted to stay here for old times' sake." He glanced at her. "When I was a kid, you know. All the times..."

"I understand. Not for *our* old times. You forgot *those*, I guess."

He didn't respond right away, but leveled a gaze toward her that sparked with electricity. "No. I tried, but couldn't." He paused. "I could never forget you, Meghan."

"Could have fooled me. So, how's Texas? Did it meet all your wildest fantasies?" She wanted to stop the acrid tone of her voice, cathartic and poisonous at the same time.

"Not at all. I think I was chasing something that didn't exist." His voice scratched as he stared beyond her, beyond the balcony. "And up to now, I haven't figured out what or why. In the meantime, I abandoned the only real thing I ever had. What *we* had."

She had no words for that. No sniping retorts to show how hurt she still was. Somewhere down inside, anger still simmered. No, not anger. Anger wasn't the same as hollow brokenness. Emptiness, the loss of something pure and beautiful. Those things hurt too. But the expression on his face as she stared back at him was clear. Regret. He regretted everything. Leaving her, possibly the new job too. Could she stay angry?

"I tried to call you. After." His voice was soft.

"I know," she said. "But it was too late. You were on your way. I figured you were calling to say, *sorry it didn't work out. But it was fun while it lasted.*" The prickles returned.

Luc shook his head. "I was *not* going to say that. Try not to read my mind, since you won't be accurate." He sighed. "It took me about a week to fully see things from your perspective. How it must have looked. Twenty-twenty. Then I felt like an idiot."

She stared at him. "It took you a *week*? A week to understand that, oh yeah, we're a committed couple, dated for a year, and I should have said something before moving to *Texas*? We were committed, Luc! I was, in any case." The hurt and humiliation flooded back. She crossed her arms and turned away. "And that's when you remembered to call and say whatever you were planning to say. A week later." She shook her head. She remembered she'd already blocked him by then.

Luc fell silent. Several tense, brooding minutes passed. "I guess I was trying to prove myself in the work realm."

"Men," she snorted, then turned back to him. "At least you know what's really important, Luc. Proving yourself."

"Hey, I'm *admitting* I was trying to prove myself. I'm being vulnerable with you and you're throwing it back at me."

Poor baby. Big gold medals for being vulnerable. "And that was more important than what we'd built together." She perched forward on her chair. "I *loved* you, Luc!"

"I don't have any defense, Meghan. The worst thing against me is that I loved you too. I loved you and I still took the job. You would have understood more of my motivation if I'd talked it over with you first."

"Yes, that would have been a good start. We'd have worked it out *together*. Like couples *do*."

Luc blew out a breath of air. "Meghan, I can't undo what's been done. I've missed you. I've regretted everything. I regret. Present tense. I was a dope and a bonehead, and I lost you. Can we leave the past and all the anger behind now? Can you...forgive?"

"You mean..." Was he talking about forgiveness or getting back together? Her heart started pounding again. No, she wasn't ready to just pick up where they left off. Was she?

"Start over by not being mad anymore," he supplied, likely seeing where her mind was traveling. "Your grudges are legendary, and I'd like to encourage you to give up this one. What's the use of staying angry?"

"No use." She fell back against the chair and crossed her arms. "No use at all." True, her grudges had only made her miserable. And as a daughter of God, did she really want to have that reputation? World medal in grudge-keeping? She sighed. "Yes, Luc. I'll try to forgive you."

"Try?"

He cocked his head and smiled at her. Darn it all. He was still incredibly handsome. And her inside response—like warm melting sugar plus a few butterflies—wasn't helping matters. "Yes. But what makes this hard is that me saying I forgive you will just make you feel all better, but you still ruined my life." She turned away. Her eyes stung as the reality of her statement brought back a tide of broken dreams. She'd assumed they'd get married then suddenly, it was over.

The sting in her eyes turned to tears rolling down her cheeks. Oh, no, no. Not the time for tears. But she couldn't help it. She'd gone from angry to weeping. Why couldn't she stay mad at Luc? Anger put her in a much stronger position than weeping did. Weeping made her feel small and helpless, rejected, forgotten. Like she'd felt when her sisters took off somewhere together without her. The grudge gave her power over all that.

"Hey." She felt his hand on her arm, his voice gentle like silk.

She stood and backed away. Next thing, he'd give her a nice, comforting hug as if he weren't the one who'd broken her heart in two. As if he could now go on in his life, released from his burden of guilt. Once Meghan forgave him, he'd feel lighter, happier. He could return to Texas feeling cured of being a jerk. Then go on and be a jerk to the next woman until he'd *proven* himself. To himself.

"Okay, you can go now, Luc. I'll try to forgive you, and you try not to do this to another woman you say you love. All will be well. Go ahead, be happy and carefree." She went inside but couldn't stem the tide of tears. The ground inside her crumbled, and she couldn't do a thing about it but fall into the crevasse.

As she sobbed next to the kitchen counter, she felt his presence behind her.

"I'm sorry I've brought all this up, Meghan, by being here. If you want, I'll leave, and you won't have to see me anymore."

His words caused a chill inside. Is that what she wanted? She shook her head. "That's not what I want, Luc. I'm just...reacting. It's intense, seeing you again. You hurt me more than you can even imagine.

And it was all nothing to you. A job. You left us for a job."

"That's where you're wrong. It wasn't nothing. It's never been that. You're the only woman I ever loved."

She whirled around. "Then why did you put the job first?" She flicked her hand. "No, we've already talked about that, and you don't know. So, forget it." She grabbed a tissue and mopped her face, then turned to him. "What's next with the thing your grandmother needs?"

A long silence dominated the room. "I need to come back once more. I can call you and let you know I'm coming. That way, you don't have to be here. Or..."

"Or?"

He offered a tiny smile. "Or you can help me find it. It's a diary my grandmother wants to see again before...before she leaves. We can look for it together. Maybe two sets of eyes are needed here. And I remember you're gifted at this kind of thing."

Meghan crossed her arms. "I am, huh? Give me your number and I'll think about it. I'm still on vacation, you know."

"I know. You might not want to spend one of your vacation days rooting through a closet full of boxes. But if you do, I'd like that."

They exchanged numbers, then she walked him to the door.

He faced her, seeming to search for words. He raised one hand as if to touch her, but let it fall. His face was more solemn than she'd ever seen it. "I'm really glad to see you, Meghan. Despite everything."

She didn't respond but held his gaze for a long moment, then opened the door. He slipped out onto the landing, and she closed the door behind him.

He was glad to see her. That was something, though what did it mean? Despite knowing he was in Nice, seeing him sent her emotions spiraling into a confused mess it might take time to untangle.

Chapter Eight

After the door shut behind him, Luc stood immobile on the fifth-floor landing. He tried to sort his thoughts, and what felt like metal towers falling inside him, destroying his image of himself and life as he knew it. He struggled to breathe. Surrounded by identical doors extending down the hall, glimpsing the shiny silver elevator around the corner... he saw only her imprinted on his mind.

What had just happened? He'd seen Meghan Clark in Nice. First time in a year and a half. And she looked amazing, every bit as beautiful as she'd been in his memory. Even with rumpled hair (especially with rumpled hair), rumpled clothing, and large brown doe eyes expressing the depth of her hurt. After all the time...hurt *he* had put there.

How could he have hurt her like that? This woman he'd missed every day since then? It was all he could do to keep from knocking on the door and taking her in his arms. Telling her he'd been a fool, and could they please start over.

But he couldn't. He'd messed up and *bad*. She probably didn't even believe that he had loved her. And still did. Did he have the time to prove it before she returned to...wherever she lived now? Would she ever believe him again?

Luc forced himself to head toward the elevator, his feet like lead boots. He'd pray that she'd be willing to work on the closet project with him the following day. Just to have more time with her. He couldn't let her go yet, but didn't know if there was any reason to hope. When everything fell apart, it had taken him a week to realize the gravity of what he'd done. But there was no measuring the gravity he felt now. His heart matched the descending elevator in its freefall.

So, he walked west on Rue Cassini until it changed names. Twice. He found himself near the Gare SNCF train station and prayed the whole way. He prayed to have a shot with Meghan again if God willed it, but he also prayed he could figure out what kind of rocks were in his head. Why did he need to prove himself to the point of ruining his future with Meghan? Sounded stupid when he'd said the words to her, and she hadn't let him slide. No, she'd mocked him. And she'd been right. A child of God who had to prove himself to *that* point? How did he get such a tattered sense of who he really was? Of the man God had made him to be?

He turned south and kept walking all the way to the waterfront. Late afternoon clusters of vacationers filled both the wide Avenue des Anglais and the beach, which consisted of round stones instead of sand. During his childhood, those stones had always amused him, especially the musical sound they made when the waves sluiced back and forth over them.

A few seats on the white benches facing the Mediterranean sat empty. He plopped down on one of them. Turquoise waters mesmerized him as his thoughts continued to chew away, like the waves, back and forth. The ironic thing was the emotional price he'd paid to get the job in Texas and the low payout he experienced there. He'd been unable to make friends or find any leisure or social settings that he enjoyed. His apartment was blah. Couldn't find a church home where he fit. The work itself was challenging in a good way. He pushed himself and had a measure of satisfaction. But it would be easy to find similar work in dozens of places he liked better. And he could have done all that without leaving Virginia. Without losing Meghan.

There was a good reason people said hindsight was twenty-twenty. Because of all the kicks in the hind parts when one made a dumb decision.

The following morning, Luc awakened early, despite a fitful night's sleep. He waited until a reasonable hour to call Meghan. While he nursed a second espresso on the balcony, he prayed she'd consent to help him with the journal project. Or diary, or whatever it was. The task he was suddenly thankful for.

"Good morning, Luc." The sound of her voice on the phone shot him with adrenaline. He combed it for warmth and found a trace. Or maybe it was indulgence or pity. As long as it wasn't tears or hostility, he'd take it.

"Hi, Meghan. I hope you slept well. So, I was thinking about my task. I'd be grateful if you'd help me out, but it doesn't have to take the whole day. I *do* remember you're on vacation. What do you think?"

"Okay. I'll help you. What time do you want to come?"

"Whatever works for you. Nine? Ten?"

"Ten works. I'll see you then." He disconnected and let out the breath he'd been holding. Then pumped his fist.

Now he wasn't sure he wanted to find *Mamie*'s journal on the first try. If they did, then he'd come up with some other way to spend time with Meghan.

He arrived at the Cassini apartment right at ten and rang the bell. When Meghan opened the door, her hair and clothing weren't rumpled, though she'd still dressed casually. And she still took his breath away.

They stared at each other for a long second. "Want to come in?" She stepped back and Luc slipped into his apartment for the third time that week. And for the first time, knowing Meghan Clark was inside. He had never been tongue-tied around Meghan, but that day he came close. Loads of water flowed under their romantic bridge. It was hard to know where to start. He'd already made the apologies. He'd just take it slowly.

"Want some coffee?" she asked. "It's not espresso. It's drip." She went to the kitchen, and he followed. He watched her as she reached for the carafe and poured some into her cup.

"No, thanks. I had two at home."

"Where are you staying?" She blew into her cup and took a sip, looking completely composed compared to yesterday.

"I have another apartment. Well, Max and I own it together. I'm staying there."

"Is that the apartment you wanted me to go to the second week? I recall you had another one."

"Yeah. It's nice. A little farther from the waterfront, but it's a big one. Three bedrooms and a huge kitchen."

"Did your grandmother give you that one too?"

"She split it between Max and me because of the size. She always wanted to keep everything fair."

"What about the place she currently lives? Is that yours too?"

"No, I'm not sure what her plans are for that one. Maybe my dad, though they fell out a few years back and they don't speak."

Her brow furrowed as she cradled her cup. "Even though she's about to die? Wouldn't they make amends?"

He shrugged. "That's between them. Neither one of them talks to me about it, though *Mamie* and I are close."

"Yes, I remember that. It must be hard for you to lose her." Her businesslike demeanor cracked, and what looked like genuine sympathy leaked through.

Luc looked at his hands. "She's pretty special. But she's at peace. And she's had a good life."

"I wonder what she wants with the book. The diary." Meghan's sudden smile disarmed him, her deep dimples embellishing her cheeks. He'd always loved those dimples. "Even if we find it," she continued, "we can't read it. It's private. She might choose not to tell you."

He closed some of the distance between them and leaned against the opposite counter. "Then that would be her choice. There may be some secret there she's forgotten or something she remembers she wants to reread one last time. Like an old love letter from *Papi*, or someone before him."

Meghan's eyes widened. "Really? Before your *Papi*? She'd think of that other person on her deathbed?"

Luc laughed. "Meghan, I have no idea. She might tell us, you know, as compensation for finding it."

After a moment of silence, he hitched his head toward the back of the apartment. "Do you want to get started?"

"Sure." She took another sip and strode purposefully toward the closet as if she owned the place. She stood back while Luc unlocked the padlock and swung the door open.

She scanned the contents. "It's pretty full. I can see why you didn't find it with just a couple quick stopovers."

"Yeah, I was being completely unrealistic. Along with not very thorough."

"How much of this is yours and how much is hers? And who else's?"

Luc stepped inside, his hands shoved deep into his jean pockets, and scanned the metal shelves that reached almost to the ceiling. "About two-thirds of it is mine. I always had this idea that I'd come more often and didn't want to start from zero. Remember when we were here, we had all this stuff already? Kitchen stuff, beach stuff, picnic stuff..."

Meghan's expression chilled, likely at the mention of their romantic week two years earlier. "Seems like you wouldn't need all this when you've got a fully stocked kitchen." Her frown looked disapproving. "And you didn't come back as often as you thought."

"No, not since you and I were here. When *Papi* died and *Mamie* moved to Beaulieu, she got rid of most the things she didn't want to take with her. But there were just a few things she'd wanted to keep here, mostly old mementos, I think."

"Doesn't she have storage where she is?"

"Yes, she does. My guess is there are certain things she never wanted my dad to find, even if he inherits her apartment. In that case, he'd have access to everything, whereas I'd be the only one who'd have access here."

"Ah. That's very likely her motivation. Makes total sense. And it's smart. A way of controlling who sees what, even after she's gone."

Meghan stood beside him, coming up to his shoulder. He could still smell her citrusy shampoo, and it unleashed a flood of memories. Made him want to close his eyes and just inhale. Inhale and remember. And try not to weep.

He pulled his attention back to the task. "I suggest we take one shelf at a time. What do you think? Be systematic?"

"We can each take a box and go through it. Some boxes are cardboard, and you may want to re-tape them when we're done. Do you have tape?"

"Sure do, but it's probably in one of the boxes." He lifted his brows playfully.

She shook her head. "How practical. Well, let's get started."

Luc reached above her head to pull down the smaller boxes on the top shelf. "One for you and one for me." He set them on the floor. "We can sit on the floor or bring each box out to the dining table."

"Remind me what we're looking for. A small book, like a diary? Or something bigger?"

"Smaller. She said it has flowers on the cover. She also thought it was in a box with a purple handle. A detail she forgot to mention when I came the first time."

Meghan surveyed the shelves. "At first glance, I don't see purple anywhere. Maybe it'll be behind another box. It's helpful that most of this is stacked on shelves instead of all over the floor. Otherwise, we'd be here all day."

Sounded good to Luc.

"I assume your boxes are distinct from your grandmother's, right?" Meghan asked. "Can you identify yours from hers?"

"Um...I hope so. Once we open a box I'll know right away if it's hers or mine."

They decided to take the boxes to the dining table, in case they had to empty the whole thing. And until they found the diary, that's what they'd do.

"I think everything on the top of the left shelf is hers," Luc said. "We'll start there. I remember now that I'd separated them a certain way."

"I'm glad you did." Meghan was already shuffling through papers and booklets. They looked like recipes. Nothing resembling a flowered diary. "This is pretty interesting," she said. "Newspaper clippings from the war, and here's some from De Gaulle, more from the fifties." Her gaze met Luc's. "I wonder if she'd enjoy seeing these too."

Luc shrugged. "She didn't ask for them. I say let's look for the diary and when we find it, we put everything back and forget that closet. We can't second guess what she'd want to see. She's hardly even awake much these days."

Meghan frowned and her eyes drooped, as if the reality of his grandmother's health was finally hitting her.

They worked silently for a few minutes, though Luc glanced at her now and then, still unable to believe he was in Nice working peacefully on a project with Meghan. God was good. He was the only one able to pull something like this off, bringing him to Nice at the very moment she was there. At least he hoped it was divine intervention, which meant there might be some kind of happy outcome in the offing.

"I'm finished with this one. It was interesting to get glimpses of your grandmother's life, but I didn't find our elusive diary." She snapped down the plastic handles and returned the box to its shelf, then brought another one to the table. "What if it really isn't here? We might not find it."

Luc twisted his mouth. "That's a chance we're taking. But at least we'll know. And it put us back into touch. That's something."

She met his gaze. "Not sure what, though," she murmured, as one corner of her mouth quirked.

"Don't you know?" He swallowed his next words...*God is giving us a second chance.* He wanted her to be ready for the words, receptive to them. In a few days, they'd both know. He hoped he had that much time.

"Where do you live now?" His sudden change of topic would reroute the conversation until they were both more prepared. Aside from that, he was curious. "I figured you moved."

"Atlanta." She pried off the top of the plastic bin. "I got a new job at an event company. It's more interesting than human resources."

"Did you...leave immediately after we broke up?" He saw her flinch. "I mean, when did you move there?"

"A few months later. I've been there about a year."

"Do you like it?"

"I do. Just not sure I'll stay in Atlanta. Housing is expensive, and I had to start over...socially. I have a couple friends from work, though."

Was she steering him away from curiosity about her love life? "Dating anyone?"

Her jaw hardened. "I just broke up with someone." She shrugged as if it didn't matter. "You?"

"No." He didn't know what else he could say. *No one was like you* wouldn't sound sincere to her, even if it was the cry stuck in his throat.

Nothing in his box. He stood, resealed it, and swapped it for a new one. "I'm noting how many of these belong to *Mamie*, because when she's gone, I don't plan to keep all this."

"I don't blame you, though you should keep some things for your children. I mean, your future children. They'd want to know their great-grandmother."

"You think?" Women had a weird way of thinking. That would never have crossed his mind.

"Of course." She blew out an impatient puff of air. "Families are important, even if they're gone. It's called *heritage. Ancestry.*" She waved some old postcards at him.

Luc grinned. "If you say so."

"Men," she muttered and shook her head.

"You keep saying that. We're not that bad."

Meghan only huffed and kept looking through the box in front of her, though he detected a smile creeping onto her lips. "Why aren't you dating anyone?" she finally said, though didn't meet his gaze.

"Uh, well like I told you yesterday, I was in love with *you*. I know you think that's incompatible with moving. A man would understand. Since we're so weird and different in the way we think."

"You can say that again."

He shrugged.

"I work a lot. I don't socialize much."

Meghan leaned back and crossed her arms. "I seem to remember your habit of working much more than you need to, for whatever reason." She stared at him. "My guess is," she added more softly. "You're not that happy there."

"And you'd be right."

She blinked during a pause. "No comment."

Silence returned as they completed the second set of boxes and tackled a third. "How long should we go at this?" He broke the long silence of concentration. "I know we haven't finished, but we can do some today, then some tomorrow, so you don't feel like you'd spent your whole vacation in the closet."

"That's good of you." Her dark eyes held a challenge. "Very considerate. We'll do one more. Then take a walk."

"Together?" Hope spurted in his chest. "I'd like that," he added before she could tell him she preferred to walk alone.

ल ल ल

They'd agreed to sort through half of Isabelle's boxes before stopping. At that point, they hadn't found the diary. "That means we'll for sure find it tomorrow," Meghan said.

"Or else we'll have to tell *Mamie* she was mistaken, and it's not there." Luc stood to stretch his lanky frame, then stacked the boxes. "She won't be able to tell me to come back again, because we'll have gone through *every* box in the closet that's hers."

"Right. Is there any chance her book is in one of *your* boxes?"

"No." Luc groaned. "*Probably* not."

It was fun doing a project with him, easing into being around him again without fighting about the past. It came up in shadowy references once in a while, but how could it not? But at least her anger had ebbed away. Maybe she *could* forgive him.

At least he wasn't dating the six-foot blonde supermodel. Or anyone else. Why would Meghan be relieved? Did she want him to feel as jilted as she did, or was she hoping they'd have a shot at part two?

She shook away those thoughts. They'd just muddy the waters, and she didn't need that. Yet, she had to admit, her skin tingled around him, and she kept noticing little things she'd always loved. The greenish hazel of his eyes that shifted shades in different light, the almost sandy brown hair, thick and wavy, with blond highlights. She'd always been thankful he hadn't adopted the super-short hairstyle popular with many French young men. She liked enough hair on a man to sink her fingers into and see it curl around his neck.

Could she really risk her heart again to Luc Badaux?

"Time to call it quits for today," he announced, breaking into her thoughts.

"Okay. We'll finish tomorrow?" She wriggled out of her seat and stood.

"If you're game. When are you free?" He took a step toward her.

"Hmm. I want to spend the morning at the market on Cours Saleya, then sit on the beach some. Let's meet around three tomorrow. I bet we can finish up."

Luc nodded. "Sounds good. Uh... Still up for taking a walk together"

"Of course. It was my idea." She kept her words casual, though her heart raced. He wanted to spend more time with her. He didn't only want her help with the task. "I'll let you lead. You're the Nice expert, after all."

He bestowed a lop-sided grin, and it drew her in. He stood close to her, her eyes strayed to an even row of white teeth and his famous lips... She'd always had such a weakness for Luc Badaux. She swallowed and shifted her gaze to the table where they'd worked.

"How about we climb to the top of the Parc de la Colline du Château. Remember that?"

"Up on the hill? Yes, I remember. Isn't there also an elevator?"

"You are correct. We'll take it, then climb down. You don't want to miss your iconic photo of the Nice shoreline from up there, do you?"

"Not a chance." She walked to the couch to retrieve her sneakers. "What about lunch? I'm hungry."

"Me too. I'll get us some socca to take with us."

"Um, remind me..."

"It's the chickpea crêpes Nice is known for. You loved them, remember?"

"Oh, yes! I remember. They're amazing." At his reference, sadness swelled briefly inside. Then she reminded herself she was here in Nice with Luc Badaux. "Sounds great."

The enticing fried aroma of a bag full of socca filled the small elevator as it rose to the summit of the hill. It was a must-see destination, with stunning views, and a small bubbling waterfall on the way down.

Once out of the elevator, they followed the path until it led to the top of the hill. Luc led her to a bench overlooking the city and the shimmering water below. "I bet Atlanta can't compete with this for a picnic spot."

"I'll have to agree with you. This is spectacular. I'll be right back." She went to the railing and fished her phone from her backpack. She'd taken several shots of the vista and shoreline before she felt Luc beside her, standing close enough to touch her arm.

"Want me to take one of you?" His voice was soft, inviting. Probably meant nothing.

"Sure." She posed by the rail. "Get the background."

"I will, though you're just as beautiful." He stepped toward her and returned her phone. "Just as beautiful as ever, Meghan."

She took a coy voice. "Are you flirting with me, Bad Boy?"

A smile toyed with a corner of his mouth. "Just a little. And telling the truth."

"Can you say that in Texan?"

"Ahm tellin' the tuh-rooth." They laughed. "How about we get a selfie?"

"I'll have to delete it later if it makes me sad."

"You won't want to delete this." He stood close to her, his cheek nearly touching hers, and took a selfie of the two of them jammed together with a swath of blue water in the background.

"You sound so sure." He returned her phone, and she peered at the photo. Their faces looked enormous but happy against the background of sky and water. "No one will believe this picture. I'll have to point out to people that it's from *this* year."

They returned to the bench. Luc prayed for them, including thanks for the circumstances that allowed their paths to cross. Meghan couldn't help but agree, though she didn't know where it was leading. To more hurt, to a platonic friendship, to being forgotten once she got back on the plane?

Eat your socca and live in the moment. You don't know what God has up his sleeve.

Chapter Nine

Luc waited promptly at three o'clock the next day. When Meghan opened the door, her facial expression was warmer than the day before. And her nose was redder.

"Did you wear sunscreen today?" With a smile, Luc brushed past her.

"I did this morning, but forgot to reapply it. Am I red?"

"You have a very cute red button nose. Did you enjoy the *marché* and the beach?"

"Yes, very much. I love the energy of the market at Salaya. I got a lot of things for salads this morning, and then..." She walked to the couch where a paper bag sat. "I couldn't help myself." Meghan reached in and drew out a round Jacquard tablecloth in turquoise and yellow Provençal designs.

"I recall you bought one of those when we were here together."

She held it out in front of her. "I'm building a collection. And I had to get a bag of herbes de Provence."

"Very important." He gave her an indulgent look. "I also remember how much you enjoy shopping. Especially for little, inexpensive things."

She smiled at his comment. "You remembered. I *do* enjoy that. Fun little items and French toiletries. I *love* them. The tablecloth wasn't inexpensive, though. Two weeks in Nice is costing me enough."

Luc gave her an exaggerated bow. "The owner thanks you. You're helping him pay his bills in Texas."

She made a face. "Anytime. Let's get to work, Bad Boy."

He chuckled as he strode to the closet and opened the padlock.

Like the day before, they settled at the dining table and spread out the contents of their boxes. "I hope we don't get all the way to the end and see that it isn't there." Meghan pulled papers from the box and stacked them according to size.

A few minutes later, she stood. "Want something cold to drink?"

He nodded, and she brought a pitcher of water and two glasses from the kitchen. "I forgot my manners. I should have asked when you arrived." She poured the water and sat down, but didn't resume her work. "Can I ask you something?"

Luc met her gaze and braced himself for her question.

"When you accepted the job in Texas without telling me about it ahead of time, what were you assuming would happen between us? Did you figure you'd break up with me because you were moving, or that we'd do long-distance?"

Though it was a good question, Luc knew his answer wasn't a good one. She'd likely get angry and throw him out if he told her. It was a lose-lose, yet she waited for his response, her large brown eyes expectant. He took a breath and decided on the truth. "When I was growing up, our family moved a few times. Usually not too far, until we moved to the States. But the reason we moved was always my dad's job. He made more money, had more of a career type job than my mom. She just followed along. They moved because of his job, and we all followed, regardless of how we felt about it. That was the pattern I grew up with. It was a foregone conclusion that the husband's job was more important."

"But we weren't married or even engaged." Meghan shifted weight on her elbows against the table. "Why would you assume I'd quit my job and follow you? I'd have had to get a new job in Texas, and that was no guarantee."

The gentleness of her voice took him by surprise. He might be brave enough to tell her the truth. "You're right. I wasn't considering you enough. I didn't even think about whether it would be easy for you to find something or not. I wish I'd done things differently."

She blinked. "How would you have done it differently?"

That was easy. He'd pondered that question about eight thousand times. "The first thing I'd have done is think of *us,* not the job. And my feelings for you. I actually *did* picture you coming with me, but assumed you would instead of asking you to. And I wondered if I was ready to propose."

Meghan's mouth dropped open, then she lowered her eyes. "Boy, did you screw *that* one up."

"I'm well aware. You found out about the job before I'd decided how I was going to handle telling you. And that was unfortunate. I didn't have a chance to propose, or to explain about the job. I knew the offer would push me to decide one way or the other, but I didn't know if I was ready for engagement." Hurt passed across her face. "Don't get me wrong, Meghan. I felt we were moving in that direction. I wanted to marry you, but I didn't know if the timing was right or if we were ready."

He took a long sip of water to buy time, to unscramble his thoughts and words, and to cool his face from the effort of admitting what he'd told no one else. "So, if I could do it again, I'd sit down with you and tell you about the job offer."

And he'd have proposed. He'd thought about that aspect dozens of times since. He might not have felt ready, but would have dived in, pushed by circumstances to do what he knew was only a matter of time. One thing that had stopped him was the risk of her thinking the proposal was because of the job, instead of his true desire. No way to win that one.

"Career-wise, it was a good move for me," he continued, "But I would want us to decide together what we'd do, whether I would accept it or not, and how our relationship would work with that, whether we'd do long distance for a while, or something else."

"Or you could have turned the job down. You told me you weren't unhappy at your job in Virginia."

"True. I could have stayed there. That's about all I can say, Meghan. I wish I'd done things differently."

She sighed and her gaze drifted beyond his head. "Me too. Thanks, Luc. I was just curious, and that helps. It helps me to know you didn't just toss me out of consideration and leave me behind."

"No, Meghan. I didn't do that." He took her hand across the table. Her gaze darted to their clasped hands, then back to his eyes. "You had every right to be curious about my messed-up thought process. I'm so sorry. I'm sorry about the way things turned out. It was a loss for both of us, because we had something special." *And yet we're here together now...*

He released her hand. Her frame seemed to shrivel in her chair, like a balloon releasing its last breath of air. "I'm done with this one." Meghan stood and took the box to the closet, a dejected shuffle to her step. She returned with another one and pried open the lid. She stared inside. "Luc, there's something purple *inside* the box. I can see the edge. I wonder if that's it." She moved a couple of ceramic knick knacks aside and set several packets of letters wrapped in ribbon on the table. "Here it is. Could this be the purple thing she's thinking about? It's not a handle. Seems to be a box."

The intensity of the conversation had shifted to banal. He wasn't sure how he felt about that. He'd almost been on the verge of proposing right then.

Meghan removed the cover of the box with her fingernails. "This is it, Luc. Your grandma's diary." She held up a small book, about an inch thick, with faded lilies on the worn fabric cover. A small brass lock held it closed. Locked, as *Mamie* had predicted.

"*Enfin! La réussite!*" he called out. "We succeeded!" He held up one hand for her high-five, wishing he were close enough to hug her. Darned table in the way. Maybe he could sneak one later.

"I have an idea. Well, two." He stood. "Come with me to *Mamie*'s tomorrow and we'll give it to her together." He circled the table until he stood next to her.

Meghan smiled. "Yes, absolutely. I'd love to see her again. What's the second idea?" She pushed back her chair and stood.

He reached out and tucked a lock of hair away from her face. He was inches away from her. Their eyes locked, and a hum rumbled deep inside him. Oh, how he wanted to kiss her then. "The second idea," he said softly, "is I take you to dinner to celebrate and to thank you for your efforts."

"Deal." She took a step back. "Let's get all this cleaned up and we can get out of here. The sun's still out."

He smirked, unsure what to make of her sudden physical distance. "I like the way you think, Miss Clark."

༺ ༺ ༺

"Give me a few minutes to change clothes, since we're going out." Meghan slipped back into the bedroom before Luc could respond. Her heart thumped in her chest. She wiped perspiration from her forehead and stared in the mirror at her flushed face. Not from sunburn.

Things had gotten steamy *real* quick, and they'd hardly touched. But it had always been like that between them. Instant steam with just a look, a word, a touch. Amazing they'd kept themselves out of the bedroom while they dated, but they had. She would have thought being separated for so long would cool her racing blood to cynicism, hurt, or indifference.

His words had caressed her scar tissue deep in its cavern. He'd assumed she'd go to Texas with him, as his fiancé, or serious girlfriend. He *had* considered her, but had botched the communication. And since the day they broke up, she'd felt the opposite of what he'd intended. She'd felt discarded, forgotten. But with his words, those feelings splintered and drifted away. Mostly. It would still take time. But the lightness that remained felt clean and renewed.

Meghan went to the closet and surveyed her cotton sundresses. She chose one that had been Luc's favorite, red with tiny yellow hearts. She'd told him once that each tiny heart represented her love for him, like a thumbnail of something larger. Her choice would say something to him. Or not. But that was fine, because she liked it.

Wedge sandals, feminine yet comfortable, and a straw hat. They'd worked all afternoon on Isabelle's request, and now they'd enjoy the town. Together. Meghan and Luc. How unexpected was *that*?

She emerged from the bedroom and his eyes widened faintly. He remembered. If she had any doubt, the slow smile and focused gaze convinced her. She slipped her purse over one shoulder, and they left the apartment.

The elevator reached the ground floor, and they emerged onto Rue Cassini. "I'd like to call *Mamie* and let her know we found her diary," Luc said. They returned outside, and he tapped what she guessed was his grandmother's number. He spoke in French, a sound she never tired of hearing—not just anyone's voice, but Luc's—then disconnected.

"She wasn't there?" Meghan asked.

"She's sleeping. I told her caregiver to pass along the message that we found the diary *and* that I had a surprise for her."

"Me?" Meghan cocked her head.

"You. She thought I was nuts for letting you go."

"You were definitely that." She batted her eyes for effect. "But then, I always knew your grandmother was smart."

"You're mighty agreeable today. When it comes to my failings." Luc grinned and started walking. Soon they arrived at the lively Garibaldi Square. To one side sat a stately Belle Epoch building that looked like a lavish hotel from the nineteenth century.

"How beautiful. What is it?" Meghan asked.

"That's the natural history museum. You can see a full dinosaur skeleton in there. And lots more. Over there is the modern art museum." He pointed to a structure that was as creatively modern as the other was historic. "In case you want to take in local cultural things. They're not too far to walk from the apartment."

"Only if it rains." Meghan stretched her arms and fingers. Felt good. "I want all the French sunshine I can get."

"That would be me, I'm pretty sure."

Meghan swatted his arm, but she was smiling. "Just because I forgave you, now you're full of yourself. A regular comedian."

He stopped. "You forgave me?" His face was solemn.

"Yes, Luc," she whispered. "You're off the hook."

Without a word, he leaned forward and kissed her forehead. Then turned and kept walking.

She liked his gesture, but hoped he hadn't taken her forgiveness lightly. For sure, she hadn't given it lightly. Her forehead tingled from the sudden kiss.

Meghan strolled beside Luc as he turned to a narrow medieval-looking street leading to the Old Town. Tall pastel buildings crammed together on the tiny street cast long shadows on the merchants below. Their displays filled the cobbled paths, as did the rumble of conversations and the aroma of gelato cones and roasted pralines. They stopped and took some samples from the praline store, then browsed at a few more shops.

"Do you need to get gifts for anyone?" Meghan asked.

"Nah. The person I'm closest to now is Max, and he'd laugh me out of the room if I got him a Nice T-shirt. Although I could get him a lavender sachet, just to tease him."

Meghan laughed. "I think you should do it. I'd love to see the look on his face." She shook her head. "Guys and girls are *so* different."

"What about you? You're not French, so it's different with your family. You might want to bring them all kinds of souvenirs. An apron for your mom, lavender stuff for your sisters."

"I...I don't really have a close relationship with them."

"Still?"

Shame rubbed inside. "Yeah. I guess I keep everyone at arm's length. I need to make more effort, or I won't ever know my nieces and nephews *or* my sisters. We live far from each other, but that's no excuse."

"You're right, Meggie." He'd taken her father's nickname for her, and somehow it touched her. "No excuse. I'm serious. It's the grudge, isn't it? Like with your mom?"

Meghan sighed, wanting to change the subject. Yet moved with the reminder that Luc knew her so well. "I need to let her off the hook too."

"Life's short, Meghan. She's happy, your dad's happy. Is he still in Myrtle Beach, fishing every day and eating seafood with his new wife?"

"Yeah, he's pretty happy now. He had a minor heart procedure just last week, but he's fine. Recovering at home." *She* was the only one still affected by the grudge.

Her gaze sailed over his head. "Look, there's an apron I can get for my mom. Glad you mentioned it." And postcards. She zipped into a shop to change the subject. And to take a first step toward restoring closeness with her mother.

It was almost the duplicate of a day they'd spent together two years earlier, before the hurt and separation. Almost, but not quite. At the current moment and circumstance, Meghan didn't know what it meant to walk through Old Town with Luc. She didn't know Luc's intentions or current feelings for her, or if he even had any. She used to be able to read his expressions, but either he was hiding them, or his feelings for her had gone shallow. The thought was unsettling. But what did she expect after so much time? And since she shut him out?

What did she want *now*? She was afraid to answer that question.

When they emerged from the labyrinth of the Old Town, they were close to the waterfront, so they strolled along the broad concrete promenade parallel to the shore. And back again. Luc told her about his life in Texas and about the missing time period she hadn't been part of. She told him about her job in event planning and the mistake that led her boss to order her to take two weeks of vacation.

Luc lifted his brows. "Wow, I wish my mistakes got that kind of response. Your boss sounds like a saint. What if the brides wanted revenge on you? *The Revenge of Frankenstein's Brides...* What if they trashed you on social media?"

"It all worked out in the end. I asked Emily about bad reviews, and she just shrugged. I want to be like Emily when I grow up. No grudges, no consequences...just grace." She let out a deep sigh. She had such a long way to go.

"Yeah. Grace is great. What would we do without it?"

That was for sure. God's grace poured out in rivers, yet she often had to dig for her own, despite the fact she'd received so much.

They fell silent, watching the waves roll back and forth. The theme of grace had snagged in her heart...Emily's grace toward her. God's grace in bringing her back together with Luc, if for nothing else, to be able to forgive him in person.

Maybe Meghan should ditch the grudges and keep a good thing going.

Luc found a restaurant under the trees at Messina Square, one he'd always loved and had taken Meghan to during their previous trip. A new memory in a familiar place. During the meal, he leaned attentively toward her, his gaze glued to hers. As if...as if he still felt something. As if he were trying to make up for something. As if they might have another chance.

The thought unsettled and thrilled her at the same time. It was too much too soon, after all the trauma in their history. Was it really that easy to pick up after a long and painful pause?

Was that even Luc's intent?

Chapter Ten

Luc and Meghan settled into their seats on the train to Beaulieu-sur-Mer. Excitement rippled inside him, not only because they'd found the coveted diary and could present it to his grandmother. Meghan sat next to him, their thighs and shoulders touching, which filled him with wonder and gratitude and no small amount of attraction.

"Don't get too comfortable," he told her. "We'll arrive in less than fifteen minutes."

"It's very close. No wonder you didn't need a car. But I guess here, people aren't as dependent on them as we are in the States."

The last few passengers dashed onto the train just before the heavy doors shut and the train eased forward. Soon, the landscape changed to scrubby coastal vegetation, then changed again as they rose above the pristine coastline.

Meghan leaned toward the window and stared out at the expanse of crystal blue. He understood how she felt, for he never tired of looking out at the Mediterranean, even in the dead of winter. He'd mostly been there in summer, every summer, all his life until adulthood snatched the privilege away.

"We have a family friend named Julien," he said. "He's given me a ride a few times since I've been here, but you're right, cars are often not necessary."

"Have you told me about Julien before?" Her dark, chiseled brows gathered.

"I don't remember. He was my grandfather's friend, then after *Papi's* death, he kept a protective eye on my grandmother. Especially as she got old and frail. She's a few years older than Julien. In my opinion, I think he had feelings for her, but she apparently didn't feel the same. She's never told me that, but I suspect."

"Hmm. Ever think of writing romantic novels?" An entrancing grin quirked her lips. "You might be good at that."

Luc laughed. "Yeah, right. The IT nerd writes a novel. That'll be the day. Before I met you, I'd have said I didn't have a romantic bone in my body."

"Really?" She cocked her head. "You became romantic when you met me?" Her voice had become feather soft.

He cut her a sly glance. "Do you need to ask? After you…Mmm…mmm." He made the same sound in his throat that he did when he enjoyed his mom's fried chicken. "I'm sure you remember the times…"

He slid one arm along the back of the seat, lightly touching her shoulder.

"Of course, I remember." A light chuckle escaped her throat, and a faint blush colored her neck. "Too much."

"I hope you had good memories that weren't trashed by the...what happened at the end." His voice cracked. "I certainly do. Too many to count." His words pried open a vault of sudden sadness and loss. Why'd he say that?

Meghan looked back at him with a pensive, vulnerable expression. He sighed. Could they get past the train wreck that their past relationship became and build something completely new?

"So, you were telling me about Julien. What became of him?"

"Ah, yes. Well, Julien lives in Villefranche-sur-Mer, which is minutes from Beaulieu where my grandmother lives. So, he checks on her, like a sort of surrogate big brother since *Papi* died . Then as her health failed, he kept my dad in the loop, that is until Dad and *Mamie* fell out. Then I was the one Julien would inform of everything, though *Mamie* and I talked sometimes on the phone."

"I remember you were closest to her of all the grandkids."

"Good memory. Look, we're here already." He didn't know if he was glad or not, but was eager to see his grandmother smile when he presented her the diary.

They passed through the tiny Beaulieu station and walked the five familiar blocks to his grandmother's building. Though it wasn't directly on the water, the picture window in the living room offered a stunning view of it. He'd always enjoyed going there, not only for his grandmother and all the memories being with her evoked, but because of the majestic beauty of her upscale building. In the last few years, however, that experience was tainted by her illness, the smell of medical products, and the transformation of the spacious living area into a hospital room.

Luc rang the bell, and the door swung open. "Monsieur Luc, Bienvenue." Brigitte, *Mamie*'s daytime caregiver, smiled warmly at both of them, then nodded a greeting toward Meghan before ushering them inside. "She just woke up, so she's a bit groggy. But she's expecting you."

He approached his grandmother's bed. "*Mamie*, are you awake? I have two surprises for you."

Isabelle turned her head, eyes tiny with drowsiness, and a small smile pulled at each corner of her mouth. "*Luc. Qui est-ce?*" Her eyes trained upon Meghan.

"She asks who you are," he whispered.

"*Mamie*, do you recognize this woman?" He gestured Meghan to approach.

"Bonjour, Madame Badaux," Meghan said. "It's very nice to see you again." She turned to Luc. "I don't remember. Does she speak English?"

"Yes, a little. She knew more in the past, but doesn't practice much."

"Méghanne. *Je vous connais.*" *I know you.* Her smile stretched farther. "You're...together. I'm...glad."

Luc chose not to correct her, but shot a glance at Meghan, who had also chosen to let it pass or hadn't noticed.

He approached his grandmother's bedside. "*Mamie*, we brought you the diary. The one you asked me to find." He turned to Meghan. She fished it from her purse and handed it to him. With bony hands, purple with distended veins, Isabelle took the small book. A peaceful smile appeared on her lips, though her eyes were still heavy. Would she tell them why she'd wanted it? Luc waited.

His grandmother tried the opening.

"Oh, *Mamie*," he said. "I forgot to break the lock. Shouldn't be too hard, though, since it's old. Want me to try?"

"Yes, before...you leave. Please. For now, sit." Her eyes sought Brigitte, who waited a few feet away. Brigitte nodded and pulled two chairs from the dining table. "*Asseyez-vous.*" She gestured to the chairs, then disappeared into the kitchen. Minutes later, she brought cold drinks and a plate of store-bought cookies and placed them on a side table.

"Meghan is here on vacation, *Mamie*. She's renting the Cassini apartment." How much should he say? The scenario that led him into contact with Meghan was complicated. He'd rather just let his grandmother think they'd gotten back together, especially since that is what she wanted. *And* he hoped it would soon be true. "Are you going to tell us why you wanted the diary so much?" He grinned at his grandmother.

She offered a weak smile in return and touched his hand. "*Non, pas encore.*" Not yet. "*Ne sois pas impatient. Je dois le lire d'abord.*"

Luc laughed. "Okay, *Mamie*. You're right. You can read it first. Then you might tell me why it was this important. Or not. It's your private book of memories." He didn't want to push her, but he *was* curious. He glanced at Meghan, who'd silently followed their exchange.

"You're right, it's her private book." Her voice was low. "We may never know. And that's fine."

During the next hour, *Mamie* asked a few questions to Meghan, which Luc translated, then translated Meghan's response. Questions about her family, her work. Her visit to Nice. He didn't mind translating, and the conversation didn't reveal that he and Meghan weren't together but had run into each other by chance. Or divine intervention, he chose to believe. Yet, his grandmother was no dummy. She was likely wondering how they maintained a relationship between Texas and Atlanta. Good question. How would they, if they resumed their romantic relationship? Illinois was even farther than Texas. He pushed the thought aside.

Luc stood. "*Mamie*, you need to rest. I'll find something in the kitchen to open your book, then we'll leave. *D'accord?*"

His grandmother nodded as her eyes closed. She reopened them and reached out to Meghan. Meghan rose and took her hand. She covered Meghan's hand with her other hand and murmured, "This makes...me happy...before I go."

Meghan looked up at him, her eyes glossy with tears. He held her gaze for an instant.

"I'll be right back." He slipped into the kitchen. What did *that* look mean? Was Meghan sad because they were playing a role in front of his grandmother? Or was she open to fulfilling what his grandmother believed about them? Or saddened by the prospect of *Mamie*'s imminent departure. Likely that.

He rummaged through the neat drawers of utensils, probably no longer used, until he found a filet knife. The tip might be sharp enough to pry the lock open. He inserted the tip into the hole where a key would go, but the clasp gave way, falling from the book. "How convenient," he murmured. He'd had visions of slicing it out of the book. He returned to his grandmother's bedside. "The lock fell away," he announced as he handed her the diary. "It must *want* to reveal its secrets one last time."

He and Meghan said goodbye to *Mamie* with a kiss on both cheeks then returned outside. "She's so sweet," Meghan said. "I'm sorry I'll never see her again." A few tears slipped down her cheeks. "It's strange, the connection I felt with her since the very first time. This is the second and last time. It's sad."

"You'll see her in heaven one day."

She offered a forlorn smile. "Yes, that's a relief. I'm glad she's grounded in her faith. It's a transition she can anticipate with joy."

"I have an idea," Luc said when they reached the Beaulieu train station. "What do you think if we get off at Villefranche and spend some time there? We can have dinner..." He watched her face and relief swelled inside when she smiled and met his gaze.

"That's a nice plan. I really like Villefranche. I loved it when we came before, I went back the other day. But I don't mind going again."

They arrived on the platform and Luc glanced at the black sign showing the arrival time of the train.

"It'll be here in five minutes." He turned to Meghan. "What else do you have on your list before you leave?"

She shifted her bag to the other shoulder. "I have two more full days, sadly. So, I've been to Antibes, Eze, Menton… I'd like to go to Roquebrune, if I can get there, since it's farther away. St. Paul-de-Vence or Grasse would be nice, but they're farther too."

"Not that far, but they're easier to access by car. I could borrow Julien's car. He wouldn't mind."

"You want…to come?" She looked surprised. Not a good sign.

"Of course I want to come. Don't you want me to?"

"Yes, actually, I do." Her sweet and sincere smile flooded him with optimism.

"Good. Since I was planning on bugging you until you said yes." He grinned.

She tilted her head, and her gaze swept his face. "I'll save you the trouble," she murmured in a flirtatious way.

The noisy arrival of the train broke the magical moment. They clambered aboard and slid into an empty bench seat. Within minutes, they disembarked in Villefranche-sur-Mer. Suddenly, they found themselves amidst a storybook landscape of orange, red, and yellow buildings scattered up and down hills, crisscrossed by cobbled alleys. The deep blue of the waterfront peeked between the buildings.

"I always loved it here," Luc said as they strolled down a flagstone path, flocked on either side by shops and displays. "It has a distinct feeling from Nice, which I also love. It's smaller, kind of bohemian in a way. That fits me."

"Yeah. Me too." Meghan sighed through her peaceful smile. "Though I think you're more bohemian than I am."

He looked at her as they strolled. "If I had to guess, I'd say France suits you."

She gave a slow nod. "I think I could live here for a while, to be honest. It would be weird to leave the States permanently. I don't think I could do that. But to come here often, or for long periods, that appeals to me."

Meghan had unknowingly described a dream he'd courted in his mind for several years now. And he had the profession, not to mention dual nationality, that would make it possible to live there and work remotely one day.

Meghan likely did *not* have that kind of job, though. Her career sounded more hands-on. He'd researched the ins and outs of working remotely, and his findings had encouraged him. But currently, he found himself in a netherworld of job confusion, especially with the new opportunity in Illinois. *And* with Meghan. His future looked like a puzzle that hadn't yet left its box...a random pile of pieces that didn't appear to fit.

"You remember that most restaurants in France don't start serving until seven," Luc said. "That means we have time to wander."

"Let's go, then. What's up there?" Meghan pointed to a higher terraced level of the town.

"That's an area called L'Octroi, where they have the weekly market. We used to come here a lot when I was a kid, just for a change from the bigness of Nice. I think my mom got tired of the same market all the time, so we'd go to all the different markets in the Provence towns around. It's such a thing here, the markets. Especially the evening farmers' markets. She was into it."

"I can see why. I enjoy it, and you can get good deals on food. Fresher than grocery stores, that's for sure."

Hmm. He could visualize her there, just like he could himself. Best not to run too fast too soon. He had a labyrinth of issues to sort out before that could ever become a reality. But it was thrilling to think about.

Up and down terraced levels of the town they climbed, stopping so Meghan could take photos. They wandered through the maze of Old Town and up the hill toward L'Octroi. Then on down to the marina and waterfront. They talked like old friends, and he fell easily into the comfortable rapport they'd had since the beginning. With her, he could be himself, drop his usual reserve.

They stumbled upon a picturesque restaurant on a pedestrian street with a view of the water. As they settled into a romantic table, the sun mellowed in the sky, casting dark streaks across the waves and down to the marina. A few persistent sunbathers dotted the pebbly beach, and a balmy breeze rustled the palm trees along the shore. Luc wished he could capture the moment in time. A moment with Meghan. A perfect moment.

Following dinner, the sun still cast light along the shore, tipping the waves with gold. They strolled past a few empty beach chairs. "Want to sit?" He gestured with one hand.

"Sure." Meghan slid into a lounge chair next to his. He shifted his chair closer to hers. As close as possible. They gazed in silence for a few moments at the undulating waves. A gentle lapping music from the water accompanied the sun's gradual descent.

"Meghan." Luc's voice broke the silence. He turned to her. "I don't think we're here by accident. Here at the same time in the same part of the world. Would you agree?"

Her eyes, dark in the dusk, stared round at him. She bit her lip, like she sometimes did when she pondered something out of the ordinary. And this fit the description. "The thought has occurred to me," she said softly. "I mean, we both believe in God's sovereignty and direction. What would be the chances otherwise that we'd meet here in this place? It's like angels pulling off a plot to bring us together."

Luc grinned. "Now who's the romantic novel writer?" He reached and entwined his fingers in hers. "I still care for you, Meghan. I...I love you, in fact. Still."

Her breath hitched, then silence for an agonizing moment. He kept his fingers wound in hers and his gaze locked to hers as on a target.

She swallowed. "I never stopped loving you, Luc. I tried to forget you." She shrugged and looked away to the water.

He placed one elbow on the metal arm of the chair, and with his other hand, gently drew her chin to face him. "Don't try too hard, Meghan." Then he leaned in and brushed her lips with his, softly, feather-light, testing her response. Her lips parted, and she moved toward him, encircling his neck with her arms. It was all the invitation he needed.

Luc drew her head with one hand and thrust the fingers of his other hand into her hair, deepening his kiss. Thirst for her overtook him. She'd always been the one, the only one. Time stood still as he kissed her, completing the circle of all the days he missed her and all the moments they'd spent together. The electric draw they'd always had for each other... Meghan pulled against him, sharing the deep parts of her soul. Refilling his well of doubt with reassurance that she was the one and that she still loved him.

They pulled apart, still close enough that he felt her breath on his face. "I can't lose you again," he rasped. "I'll do whatever it takes, Meghan. I love you."

A tender smile crept across her lips before she thrust forward to meet his lips with another hungry kiss.

ଓ ଓ ଓ

An astounding evening, completely unexpected, one that trickled desire down to her toes. Meghan looked at Luc as they walked, holding hands, still struggling to believe what was happening. Again. Luc Badaux, back in her life, saying he still loved her. She'd felt such emptiness without him since their breakup. Her flight toward a new job in a new state had been a misguided way to fill it.

How would they work things out with their jobs in different states? It wasn't the time to think about that. They'd talk, like they should have done a year and a half ago. No, talking too soon would break the spell. Might prove that all of it—seeing him, kissing him, to be a delightful hallucination and nothing more. Still, wonder and joy filled her to overflowing, joy she was afraid to trust.

By the time they reached the Villefranche train station, dusk had pulled its cover over the sinking sun, casting purple shadows across the sky and blackened sea. As they stood on the platform, Luc pulled her against him and kissed her deeply, apparently unmindful of several people milling around. It was France, after all.

On the short train ride, Meghan nestled against his shoulders. He hadn't let her hand go all evening, except to kiss her. Slowly, they walked to Rue Cassini and mounted the elevator. At her door, she melted into him, remaining in his arms for several minutes. "I'll leave you now," he murmured against her hair. "Can I pick you up tomorrow at eleven? Or later if you want. We can go to St. Paul or Grasse and stay for dinner."

She lifted her head from where it was tucked against his chest. "We'll see as much as we can. Have you already asked Julien to borrow his car?"

"He'll say yes. I'll text him when I get home. You'll be in my thoughts so much, I doubt I'll get any sleep." A tender smile tugged at his lips and his gaze plumbed hers. Then he kissed her a final time, a slow, probing kiss that made her knees weak.

"*A demain*...my Meghan." Until tomorrow.

Chapter Eleven

The next day, Luc double parked Julien's blue Renault along the sidewalk in front of the Cassini apartment. When he'd picked up the car at Julien's that morning, he'd asked Julien to call if there were any changes or updates regarding his grandmother. Luc wouldn't be able to see her that day, and felt a stab of guilt.

Meghan emerged from the apartment and slipped into the passenger side, looking beautiful in a white sleeveless dress with a yellow and white scarf around her neck. She looked French, in fact, and that thought made him chuckle.

As soon as she'd settled, he immediately pulled her toward him for a lengthy kiss. "Can't get enough of this," he murmured. He'd waited too long. Still seemed like a dream that emerged from a year of regret and longing. Was this even real? He'd better not mess it up.

"What a friendly greeting." She giggled when they pulled apart. He knew she didn't mind, since she'd clung to his neck as much as he did to hers.

"Just saying how happy I am to spend the day with you, Meghan Clark."

"Likewise, Bad Boy." She grinned and pulled her sunglasses from her purse.

Luc eased out of the city onto the highway. Forty minutes later, they approached the outskirts of St. Paul-de-Vence, a medieval walled village well-known as a haunt of nineteen-fifties movies stars, turn-of the-century impressionist artists, and modern tourists in the know. That reputation was underscored as they parked and joined the throngs of tourists milling through the narrow, cobbled streets.

After perusing the shops in the main route of the village, they climbed toward the top to see the Eglise Collégiale, the Chapel Folon, with sculptures and paintings inside, and the medieval Espéron Tower.

"I like it outside the city walls where it's less crowded. We could go there," Luc suggested after lunch on a terrace overlooking the valley. "You can see the trees and the valley surrounding the village." He'd had his fill of tourists already, and it wasn't really his thing to begin with. But Meghan wanted to see it. She'd heard about it, researched it in advance. She wanted to view the restaurant filled with impressionist paintings, though they weren't able to eat there without a reservation months ahead.

"We can do that," she said. "I'm kind of tired of tourist crowds too, but I must say, I haven't seen too many tourists in the towns I've visited, including

Nice. That was a pleasant surprise. There might be many more in June."

Now, they approached the tip of the village and stepped up to an overlook.

"I can breathe better already." Luc drew Meghan close at the half-wall, overlooking the lush green below. A wave of peace flowed through him just getting away from crowds. Meghan was the only one he wanted to be with.

Luc led her through an opening in the city wall, and they found themselves on the outer perimeter of the village. Homes along the road had been built into the wall. Here and there, stony staircases led in different directions back into the village.

He turned to her. "Want to go to Grasse? It's not far from here."

"Sure. That was on my list too."

They returned to the parking deck. "I hope you've accomplished most of what was on your list, since you're leaving soon." He meant it as a comment, an observation, but his words opened a hollow place inside. Back to reality. Back to not seeing her every day. He knew they needed to talk, and soon. The prospect weighed inside him, almost spoiling the idyllic moments with her.

"I'm trying not to think about getting back on a plane and leaving paradise." She spoke lightly, then shot him a coy glance. "Leaving you. I'll just squeeze everything out of each moment until then."

Not long after, they arrived in Grasse and parked in an underground deck on the outskirts of the city. For the next two hours, they wandered the streets, enjoying the faint flowery scent in the air from the perfumeries. They took a guided tour of a perfume factory, which was about the last thing Luc wanted to do, but it meant a lot to Meghan, so he sucked it up and went with her. But he liked the perfume she bought. Made him want to snuggle with her.

Later, as they wandered through the Old Town, his phone vibrated in his pocket. Dread leaped into his chest. Might be Julien. While Meghan explored the goods in a gift shop, he glanced at the screen and, with a wave of relief, saw it was not from Julien. It was an email from Freddie containing the job description Luc had requested. The sight of it in his inbox triggered a different kind of dread. How would he tell Meghan about this job prospect?

It'll be fine, he told himself. *Meghan and I will talk about it. I'll tell her this came about before I saw her again. She'll understand.* Luc wasn't sure, after her dramatic response to the last situation, which had been partly justified. He could easily tell her he wasn't happy in the Texas job, but she'd likely assume the door was wide open for him to move to Atlanta. Problem solved.

Up to a few days ago, Atlanta hadn't been anywhere on his radar. Might be similar to Texas, though with more trees. He didn't relish the idea of looking for work from zero, which he'd never had to do except once out of college. Headhunters always found him at the right moment.

Even prior to two weeks ago, Illinois wasn't on his mind either. But after talking to Freddie, he'd hate to give up that opportunity. Not only to live near Max and his mom, but the challenge this job represented. Seemed like his dream job, though he'd thought the same about Texas.

Was he back to his career versus Meghan? If he talked to her about his new job prospect, it would sure look that way to her. Not that they couldn't work something out, a partial remote, or something. That choice seemed unfair to him, and it made him almost grumpy.

Tension continued to send needles into his otherwise enjoyable day with her. He tried to live in the moment, trust God's leading, and believe it would be okay. He recited all the positive statements to himself to tamp down his nerves, but was only partially successful.

ര ര ര

Luc certainly had a knack for finding unforgettable restaurants. Meghan took a morsel of baguette and sopped up the sauce on her plate after a sumptuous dinner. The only thing that tainted the otherwise perfect evening wasn't anything she could put her finger on. Luc seemed tense, preoccupied. It might be his grandmother. He was worried about her, possibly feeling guilty for being with Meghan instead of at his *Mamie*'s bedside. But she sensed it was something more. Was he regretting his rash words of love and commitment? Was he backpedaling? Contemplating how to extricate himself from his lofty statements? She probably didn't have too long to wait, since she'd be on a plane again in forty-eight hours. The thought sunk a weight into her stomach.

That they hadn't talked about the future, post Nice, was unsettling, despite her claim to want to live in the moment, squeezing out the essence of her last days in France, or whatever else she'd said to lighten the discussion. The future of their relationship was the elephant in the room, at least for her. Just as it had been in the past.

And yet, she didn't want to be led by fear of a repeat performance. They both had to evaluate their jobs. Was she determined she would not leave hers? After Emily's kindness to her, she'd feel bad leaving it anytime soon. But with Luc back in her life, could she leave it, even if it meant going to Texas? To be with Luc and support his career? Was she willing to do that? Was it a foregone conclusion that she'd be the one to quit the job? *Lord, help me see this new situation clearly!*

She tried not to think about it, tried simply to enjoy the moments with him in this enchanted country. But it had to be discussed, sooner or later. Maybe he planned to work that out over the phone once he returned to Texas. But by that time, they'd both get back to their jobs, deep into work deadlines and other obligations. Would he fade out of her life, after this miraculous second chance they'd had? If they didn't talk about it first, it just might. Should she bring it up?

"It's sad that it all has to end. Back to Atlanta." Her voice came out thin and light. Immediately, she regretted her words when she saw confusion cross his face. She'd only intended to open *that* discussion.

Luc seemed to grope for words. "Your vacation is ending, but it's not the end for us, Meghan. That's not what you're saying, is it?"

"No, that's *not* what I'm saying! I'm saying I hate to leave Nice. I hate to leave…" she held up her hands, "…this. But I want to believe that even though Nice is over, *we* aren't. That we'll talk about things, you know, afterward. Or sometime."

"Of course, we will." A shadow of a smile quirked his lips, but didn't reassure her.

The server arrived with the bill. After he paid, they rose and left the restaurant. Luc fell silent. Had she just opened a can of worms? Why didn't he want to talk about it?

They sauntered toward the car as the sky mellowed to orange and blue. The streets had almost emptied, except for a few late diners, who flocked around the more popular restaurants.

"Everything okay?" she asked. "I'm sorry if I brought up something you don't want to talk about." Hurt laced her voice, but she couldn't mask it.

He stopped in the street, faced her, and took her hands. "I agree we need to talk about it, Meghan. And we can do it before you leave. Or soon thereafter. We'll work it out." His voice projected assurance.

She frowned. "Not sure why I had to be the one to bring it up."

His jaw tightened. "It's just that we're kind of in this magical time capsule. I didn't want to spoil it in advance with too much planning and discussing. And I didn't want it to remind us of our past problems, either." He turned a pleading expression to her as he stopped and moved a curl from her forehead. "I just want to treasure *now* with you."

Her shoulders relaxed. "You're right. I'm sorry, Luc. I didn't mean to be controlling. I understand fully what you're saying, and I agree. We'll have time to talk about what the future looks like for us. I guess I was afraid if we didn't talk about practical things when we were together, we might never do it."

"No, Meghan. That won't happen. It may take some time for us to figure out the details, but we won't just drift back into normal life as if this never happened." He shook his head, as if to emphasize his words. "As if I could ever forget you. I never did." He brushed her lips lightly with his. Relief surged through her.

Luc led her toward the car in the mostly empty garage and unlocked her door. He turned and took her hands again. "In the meantime, I want us to treasure this. This, together."

Meghan slipped her arms around his neck and kissed him, clinging to him, holding nothing back. He responded ardently as they stood locked together for several minutes in the darkness of the garage.

His kiss, his arms around her, expressed his love and commitment. Yet, something else hovered in his eyes. Something he wasn't telling her.

Chapter Twelve

Roquebrune-Cap-Martin was a storybook village nestled between Monaco and Menton. Luc had gone there several times with his family at various ages, and each time, he hadn't wanted to leave. Might have been the magic of a medieval castle, or the delicious crêpes they always ate at a picturesque crêperie at the foot of the hill.

Tourists hadn't overrun the village simply because few foreigners knew how charming it was. A colorful residential community more than a tourist draw, it still offered jaw-dropping scenery at every turn. Tiny, picturesque, almost undiscovered.

Perched on the side of a cliff, it overlooked the crystal blue sea, visible from many vantage points. The best view of all was from the medieval castle ramparts, where Luc stood beside Meghan, gawking at the stunning plunge down to the azure waters.

"Is this the most gorgeous place on earth, or what?" Meghan looked more relaxed than she had the previous evening. Which made *him* more relaxed. In fact, they'd had a peaceful, romantic day and ideal weather. That she was leaving tomorrow afternoon edged his enjoyment with sadness. Once she left, he'd return to looking after his grandmother, who he'd phoned a few times. She'd been sleeping a lot, but he'd spoken to her once. When Luc told her he was with Meghan, she approved in her frail yet determined way, dismissing his need to come visit that day. Which released only a portion of his guilt.

"It is. Lots of famous people discovered it way before we did, like Coco Chanel, Winston Churchill, and the French singer, Jacque Brel."

She lifted her brows. "They had good taste. I love it here."

"See over there?" He pointed to the cluster of buildings on a hill in the distance. "That's Monaco. You can see the marina and the tile roofs of houses and apartments from here. I was blessed to grow up in this part of the world, at least until the age of twelve."

"That's when you moved to Chicago?"

"Yeah. My dad's job took us there."

"If I remember, you liked growing up there, right?" she asked.

"At first, I was happy to be moving to America, which seemed exotic and exciting to me as a twelve-year-old kid. But once I got there, it took time to adjust. The culture is really different from here. And it's never fun to be the new kid. A kid with a French accent on top of everything else. But once I got into activities at school, and had some friends, it was okay. Each year it got a little better."

"But you no longer had the Mediterranean to swim in or these hilltop villages to visit."

"True, but we came every summer, so I kind of had the best of both worlds. The suburb where we moved in the States is nice, as you might remember." She'd come with him for Thanksgiving one year. It seemed like ancient history already. It might be an easy opening for him to talk about moving back to Illinois. Should he bring it up? The thought wrestled inside for a moment, then his courage slipped out the back door. Instead, he said, "Did you like it when you went there that one time?"

Meghan's brows furrowed. "I don't remember much except the anticipation of meeting your parents. Seemed like a big thing to me. You know, *meet the parents.*"

"Yeah. I kind of felt the same. *Bringing my girl home.* I was just there for a visit, about a week before I had to come here. It was my mom's sixtieth, so we had a big party for her."

She smiled. "That's nice. I liked your mom, I remember. Your dad too, though he wasn't there much."

"He's not as easy to like, but I'm working on it." Luc wondered how much she remembered of the things he'd told her about his dad.

"I'm glad you got to visit." She peered over the wall, mesmerized by the view. "Oh, look at that yacht. It's huge." A white vessel about the size of a city block inched into view.

Luc stood behind her and encircled her with his arms. She leaned against him with a happy sigh. "I wonder what your parents will think when you tell them we got back together."

"I know what my mom'll say. She'll tell me what a dope I was to let you go in the first place."

Meghan pulled his arms tighter around her. "And she'd be right. But I was a dope too. I overreacted."

"You did. You had reason to be angry and hurt, but we might have been able to work something out."

"I regret that." She turned to him and slid her arms around his waist. "But here we are. God overcame both our mistakes, didn't he?"

"He did." Luc drew her forward to indulge in a lengthy kiss.

Meghan's words lifted his mood, since she didn't consider the debacle completely his fault. His bad communication was certainly at the root of the problem, but her theatrical response didn't help them work it out. He hoped she'd learned enough about her part to respond to the new job with more calm. Whenever he found the right moment to talk to her about it.

After returning from Grasse the previous evening, he'd opened the document Freddie had sent with the details of the position. The more he read, the more excited he became about it. But what rotten timing. Would he have to turn it down to prove to Meghan he was serious about her? He sighed.

"I hope that's a happy sigh," she said. She must have noticed him sighing too much. It might be a red flag for her.

"Yes, it is. Let's go down there." He pointed to where the ancient-looking passage along the outside of the castle led to another spectacular view. They'd already seen the inside, some of the rooms restored and furnished to look like they did back in the day.

Luc checked his phone a few times, both to see if Julien had texted, and to see if anything else had come from Freddie. He hadn't had time to respond to the man, nor did he know how he'd respond. Freddie knew he was in France, and likely didn't expect anything immediate. But he checked, all the same.

"No word from Julien?" Meghan asked. "I guess that's good news. Your grandmother is hanging on."

"Yes, she must be. Want to go back down to the main part of the village? We can get some crêpes for an afternoon snack."

"Good timing. I was just craving something sweet."

Two hours later, Luc parked along the sidewalk near the Cassini apartment building. They'd returned early so Meghan could prepare for her flight the next day. Her departure was at two in the afternoon. Luc was planning to pick her up at eleven o'clock and drive her to the airport.

"I hope you'll come up and stay for a bit," Meghan said. "I'll have time tomorrow morning to finish packing. Unless you need to leave."

"No, I'd love to come up." They rode the elevator, and she unlocked the apartment.

"I feel a little melancholy right now." She gave him a rueful smile.

"I have an idea, then." He gently pushed a lock of her hair behind her ear and lifted her chin to kiss her. "Let's sit on the balcony for a while and watch the sunset. We can have a drink. Postpone the inevitable departure, or at least pretend we can." And probably talk about the practical aspects of two people in love living in two different states. Tension gripped his stomach.

He opened the French doors while she poured glasses of mineral water. She came to the balcony and sat beside him. "Just a few days ago we sat at this very spot." Meghan took a sip.

Luc chuckled. "Yeah, it was a stand-off, but we got over it." If he knew Meghan, she'd want to talk about how they were going to be together. He'd been walking on eggshells around that topic, because as soon as he mentioned the Illinois job, everything would hit the fan. At least, that was his fear because of the last time. But he needed to trust her more than that. And trust God.

"It's been a wonderful trip. Naturally, seeing you again. But aside from that, all the places I saw."

"Your boss will be happy you relaxed and got away. A real vacation."

"Yes, she will. She won't be surprised I had a great vacation. She might be surprised I'm coming back in a relationship since I just got out of one two weeks ago."

"Really? We haven't talked about that, but we should. That was recent. Sure you're ready for another one?" He gave her an impish smile.

She swatted his shoulder. "It's not another one. It's the same one I never got over. Maybe that's why I wasn't invested in the other guy."

"And maybe that's why I never met anyone interesting either."

"Want more to drink? I'm thirsty this evening. Must have been the dinner."

"No, thanks."

"Be right back."

She left the balcony and Luc pulled out his phone. He had a phone message. From Freddie. Fortunately, he hadn't heard the man call. That might have been awkward and premature. He needed to ease Meghan into that conversation.

Luc input his code and listened. "Hi, Luc. It's Freddie. I hope you got the job description I sent you last night. I know you're still out of town, but I wanted to go ahead and offer you the position. We haven't met personally, only over the phone, but I've seen your resume. Your dad vouched for your work ethic and highly recommended you." At this Luc's eyebrows lifted. An offer. A solid offer. What would he tell the man?

"Anything important?" Meghan sat next to him with a fresh glass of sparkling water. "Is your grandmother okay?"

"She's okay. Let's go inside."

They rose and left the balcony, but he left the doors open so the evening breeze could cool down the apartment. They settled onto the couch, and Luc took a long swig of water.

"So, is everything okay?" Meghan asked. "You look kind of intense all of a sudden."

He smiled at her and took her hand. "Well, I got a phone message. Let me give you some background first." He gathered his thoughts. Where to start? "So, I told you I visited my parents about two weeks ago. I was thinking how nice it was there, greener than my corner of Texas. We were sitting at dinner the first night and my dad told me about a friend of his who was looking to hire an IT guy to expand his business. He told the guy about me. Sounded interesting, so I emailed him, and we later talked on the phone." Luc watched her expression, which had gone from interest to suspicion. This would not go well.

He continued. "Sounded like an interesting job. I'd been in Texas for a while, and wanted to go somewhere else. He sent me a job description, and I was interested. So...he just left a message offering me the job."

"In Illinois?"

"Yeah. His company is based in Chicago."

"You want to go to Chicago?" Her warmth had evaporated. He hadn't noticed when she'd pulled her hand from his. Now her hands lay folded in her lap.

"Not necessarily. This job came up literally two weeks ago. Before I knew I was going to see you."

"But you want this job?"

Luc blew out a puff of air. "I don't know, Meghan. Under normal circumstances, meaning if I hadn't seen *you*, yes, I'd want to take the job. The work appeals to me, and I'd be able to get out of Texas."

She looked at her hands. "I didn't know you wanted to get out of Texas."

"I'd just started thinking about it for the first time when my dad mentioned the job. If I hadn't seen you, I'd have jumped at this job and given my notice as soon as I got back home."

"What are your thoughts now?"

"Now things are different." He slipped his arm along the back of the couch, leaning toward her. "I want you in my life, so we need to work out a solution we both like. That's one of the several options we have."

"What options *do* we have?"

"One option is to ease back into our relationship, since it's kind of new again. We'd keep talking. I think we can do the long-distance thing for a couple of months as we decide."

"We could. Then what? I'd move to Illinois and have to find a job there?"

"I didn't say that. I'm not assuming I'll take this job or that you'll have to move. Do you like your job a lot?"

Her eyes narrowed. "Yes. I've only been there a year, and would like to move up in the company."

"Okay. So, you like your job, but you're not crazy about living in Atlanta, you told me. I like my job okay, but don't like living in Texas. It might make sense for both of us to go somewhere different. As one option."

"But you'd be going to a new job, and I'd be going to...nothing."

He frowned. "It's not nothing for us to be together, is it?"

"You're assuming that you'd take the job, and I have to follow you. Isn't this like Texas all over again?"

He let out a frustrated sigh. "No, Meghan. We're talking about *options*, aren't we? That's only one option. I simply pointed out the fact that neither of us likes the place we're living. You see?"

"Yeah, I got that part." Suspicion laced her voice.

"So, that's one option. What are some others?"

"Another option is you come to Atlanta and find work there, since you seem to have an easy enough time finding positions. Or you keep your current job and work remotely, if they allow it."

"But if you don't like living in Atlanta..." And his company wasn't too keen on remote work. He'd asked that question back then.

"I like it okay, but it's expensive and I haven't made friends there. I work too much."

"We could make a pro and con list," he suggested.

She sighed. "You'd win. You already have a job offer waiting for you. That's a strong pro."

"Meghan," he said gently, taking her hand. "It's not win or lose. We're talking about options. I have not accepted this offer in Illinois. It's an option and we could pray about it. And keep talking."

"How would you stall the guy who offered you a job? Seems like to me you've already decided."

"And how do you know that?" He pushed down the impatience threatening to leap into his voice. He was trying so hard to be soft and reasonable, which wasn't his usual style, but she wasn't making it easy. Why did they absolutely have to talk about this *now*? "I already told you I haven't decided anything. I haven't told the guy anything. I just heard about his offer tonight, like fifteen minutes ago."

"I understand. But I sense you'd like to accept the job, and I don't blame you for that. But now that we've gotten back together, I would think that changes things."

"It does change things. As I said, if I hadn't seen you, I'd accept in an instant. But I can't do that, because *we* need to decide together. The thing we didn't do last time. This time will be different."

Meghan slumped back against the cushions. "Sure *feels* like déjà vu."

"The last time we had this situation, I didn't talk about it with you beforehand. That was the wrong thing to do. But we're talking now. We're not deciding anything, we're discussing. Which is exactly what you were eager to do, right?"

She shot him a grimace. "And you weren't? Would it be easy for you to drop me at the airport, leaving everything up in the air?"

"Meghan, we don't need to decide and control everything now, do we? Tomorrow you're flying home. We'll continue talking. Look, we haven't seen each other in a year and a half, and now we're trying to decide our immediate future in a matter of minutes the night before your flight."

"You have a point, Luc. I guess…" She frowned and crossed her arms. "I know I'm being pushy. But I didn't want to leave everything up in the air. In case you changed your mind or…" Her brow furrowed, then she buried her face in her hands.

Luc was at a loss. What was going on? "I told you I love you, Meghan." He softened his voice and laid one hand on her shoulder. "I also told you I don't want to lose you again. Remember that?"

She lifted her face. "Yes. I love you too. It's just that I…I'm sensitive about you putting your job before me, like you did while we dated."

"I'm sorry it was like that. I…I think I've changed since then." At least he hoped that was true.

"And I'm sorry I made you feel unimportant." He reached up to stroke a finger along her soft cheek. "That isn't how I feel. But I *do* need a job somewhere. A man *needs* to work. For his family, for himself. For his well-being. It's just a question of where."

"I understand that. I'm actually glad you feel that way about work, but you need balance, if we stay together. Too often in Virginia your work was so consuming. I always felt like I was less important to you, and when you took the job in Texas, it confirmed everything."

"You felt that way while we dated?"

"Don't you remember all the times we argued about it? I don't want to feel like I'm always less important than your work."

Luc groaned. She had a point. "Meghan, I get why Texas made you feel that way. But this is a chance to start over. We've both recognized it was divine intervention. Let's not make it difficult."

She wriggled on the couch to squarely face him. "So, what do you suggest? We go back to normal life and talk on the phone. We can even do virtual visits. For how long?"

Luc thrust his fingers into his hair. "I don't know. I'll need to make a decision about the job soon, but I want to hear your input."

"My input. Like it's going to make a difference." She stood and walked into the kitchen.

He followed her. "Meghan, we're both tired. You're leaving tomorrow. My grandmother's about to depart from this world. We have a lot on our minds, and to top it off, we've only been back together for what, three days?"

"That's true." She turned to him. "We have tons of things going on. I know I'm pushing you, and I don't mean to." She paused. "I'm feeling insecure and fearful that all this will fizzle, because I wasn't worth it to you the first time. I'm not convinced I will be this time. Maybe I want to be worth enough for you to sacrifice something. But I don't think you ever will." She turned away and rinsed her glass in the sink. "You just expect *me* to sacrifice. For the almighty career. So you can prove yourself."

Luc bristled. "That's unfair, Meghan. I haven't decided anything. This is exactly why I didn't want to tell you about the Illinois job, because I was sure it would poison the few days we had left together, and what we'd found again with each other. Let's not let it ruin this, please. We'll work it out. But we can't do it tonight in the next ten minutes." Was she waiting for him to give up the Illinois job to prove his love for her?

"Okay, you're right." She wore a defeated expression, but she'd agreed. Sort of. He gathered her in his arms. She circled his waist, but held loosely, as if she was already letting go.

Chapter Thirteen

Meghan closed the door behind Luc. Her chest already hurt. She needed to process everything, but she couldn't. Nothing had changed, except the state. From Texas to Illinois. He still preferred the job over her, despite what he'd told her.

Luc's problem was obvious. He wanted to have his cake and eat it too, as the old expression went. Just like his dad had done with his mom, who'd dutifully followed behind. But that was different. They were married and had children. Meghan wasn't married to Luc, yet he expected her to drop everything and follow him. He'd claimed it was one *option* among several. But she'd seen it in his eyes. For him, there was only one option.

Sure, she could insist he come to Atlanta. He'd gotten his job in Texas and now it was her turn. Would she do that? No. He might end up resenting her, regretting the sacrifice he'd made. Nor would she deprive him of following yet a new dream job.

Nothing had changed.

The next morning, Meghan finished packing. She checked the bathroom and under the bed, the coffee table and kitchen, to make sure she hadn't forgotten anything. A weight of melancholy slowed her steps, as well as fatigue from a poor night's sleep.

At last, she was ready. She left her keys on the table and pulled her large suitcase, full of clothes, souvenirs, and gifts, through the door and onto the elevator. Once outside, she returned to her adopted boulangerie and tried to force a cheery greeting to the woman who'd waited on her the first day. "*Je dois partir aujourd'hui,*" she told the woman, though her large suitcase beside her made her statement about leaving that day unnecessary. It was a goodbye to this stranger who'd been friendly to her when she'd just arrived, but who was already a part of her memories.

She ordered croissants and coffee and settled at a café table on the sidewalk for the last time. Observing the city for the last time. It would not be the last time, however, to block Luc from her active thoughts. Luc, who she missed already.

Meghan took her time rolling her suitcase to the tram that led to the airport. She'd be early, but that was fine. She could settle her thoughts that way. Have a margin before returning to Atlanta. And then another seven or eight hours in the plane to ponder what had happened over the last two weeks. Amazing weeks, despite everything. Then her heart would have to heal once again from Luc Badaux.

Luc started Julien's car. He texted Meghan. *I'm on my way. Traffic shouldn't be bad, so we'll make it with plenty of time. Love you.* He was eager to see her, hug and kiss her for the last time before her flight. And especially reassure her he was committed to them, and they'd work it out, despite how rigid she'd seemed the previous night. He wanted to believe she was more willing to discuss and work things out this time. They both knew it was a gift, running into each other again. They'd do what it took. Wouldn't they?

What if her only condition was for him to move to Atlanta? Was he willing to not only give up the job with Freddie's company, but move again? Atlanta was greener than Texas, but he'd been interested in living near home, being closer to Max and his mom. Was that more important than Meghan? No. He wouldn't make the same mistake twice. Asking that they give it time to think of options and work it out had been wise. Logical. She'd agreed. Sort of. But what else could they do?

He pulled up in front of the Cassini apartment, glad to have spent some time there after all. Especially with Meghan. He texted her again. *I'm here downstairs. Want me to come up? Or are you on your way down?* After a couple of minutes, there was still no answer, nor for his previous text. Another five minutes passed, and Meghan hadn't come. It wasn't like her.

Luc put on his flashers and buzzed the apartment. There was no answer. A heavy feeling teased his stomach. Was she still in the shower? Was she angry from the previous night's discussion? He was getting tired of second-guessing Meghan's responses. Once on the fifth floor, he rang the doorbell, as dread crept under his skin. When there was no answer, he let himself in.

Sure enough, the keys lay on the kitchen counter and there was no sign of Meghan. The bedroom and closet were empty. He stuffed his fingers through his hair. "Meghan! What did you do?" He stood still in the empty apartment as if in shock, unwilling for tears that taunted him to fill his eyes.

A glance at the time on his phone told him he could get to the airport and possibly intercept her. Frustration wrestled with sadness inside. He'd tried so hard to talk it over with her and not stir up the same reaction. But it hadn't worked. Once again, she'd overreacted, not given them time to work things out. She'd been convinced he'd already decided on the job.

Had she been right? Well, yes. He'd hoped she'd go along, like his mother always had. But he hadn't proposed to her. Hadn't made any promises other than the brash assurance that he'd never let her go again.

Had she overreacted? Also, yes. Same as the first time. Had he shown himself to be a different man? He paused as honesty tugged at his conscience. Not so sure. He *thought* he had. He'd been sincere. But Meghan had only seen a repeat of Texas. She'd even said it was no different. Didn't matter that he'd found out about the job before seeing her again. He hadn't decided. They hadn't.

And yet, he had.

Luc hit a traffic snag or two, due to road construction. He hoped he wouldn't miss her. And if he saw her, what would he say? Would he promise to do whatever she wanted? Was that her condition? In an instant, he saw her viewpoint as well as his own. How would they ever work this out? Unbelievable that they were at this same threshold for the second time. And again, at odds on how to cross over it.

He found parking easily in the airport lot and dashed inside. What were the chances of finding her here? He had to try. Hundreds of travelers milled around, stood in lines, rushed to ticket counters. He scanned the crowd and didn't see the short, dark-haired woman who'd stolen his heart.

Luc stopped and swallowed the painful lump that had formed in his throat. Yes, she had. Was she more important than the job? Of course. The Texas job should have shown him that. Yet, he still felt driven. It would be hard to give up the Illinois job which seemed perfect for him. What was wrong with him? He'd made the wrong choice before. Would he really do it again?

He dashed to the security line, knowing he couldn't go any farther. Again, he scanned the snaking line of shuffling passengers. He didn't see her. She must already be inside. Luc's shoulders sagged. If that was the case, it was too late.

Discouraged, Luc returned to the garage and got back into the car. He checked his phone in case she'd texted. Nothing, except a phone message from Julien.

Luc's heart raced as he punched his code into the phone and listened to the message. "Luc, your *Mamie* is bad now. You need to come, please."

I'm on the way. I'll pick you up, he texted Julien.

A few seconds later he read, *D'accord*. Agreed.

Luc's feverish thoughts bounced between Meghan and *Mamie*, then returned to his grandmother. As he approached Julien's building, he saw the older man waiting on the sidewalk. When he stopped, Julien slid into the passenger seat.

"I don't know what we'll find when we get there, Luc," he said. "You'd best prepare yourself."

Luc swallowed. "I thought I was prepared when I came. But it's always..." He didn't trust himself to say more.

"This is for you."

Julien tapped something sitting on one thigh. Luc shot a glance and saw the diary. The book that had brought him back into contact with Meghan. "She wanted you to keep it."

"Do you know if she was able to read it? I mean, before she got worse?"

A faint smile curved his wrinkled lips. "I assume so. But she wants you to keep it now. You can read it or not. In your place, I would."

"Oh, I wouldn't miss that." Luc pulled out onto the autoroute leading to Beaulieu. "I'll feel even closer to her."

"Another thing you should know, though it doesn't concern you directly. She wants to leave the apartment to your father. Since it doesn't look like he'll come in time, if at all, she signed it over to me. That way, if he wants it, I can sign it to him, and we'll still be in time to avoid the higher taxes."

Luc frowned. "That makes sense, and it was smart of her to do that. But quite honestly, I think she should give it to you."

Julien shrugged. "He's her son. If he wants it, I'll sign it over. It's about family."

Some family his father had been over the years to his own mother. Luc couldn't remember the last time he'd come to see her.

It didn't take long to arrive in Beaulieu and park. They entered her apartment, quiet and cloying, with the smell of floral cleaners and antiseptics. Luc approached her bed, expecting the worst. Instead, his grandmother was awake, but breathing through an oxygen tube. Her caregiver, Brigitte, hovered beside her, preparing her medications.

Luc rushed to his grandmother's side and took her hand. "I'm glad you're awake, *Mamie*."

"I'm...ready."

"Yes, you are," he told her, smiling despite the painful thickness gripping his throat. "Like a beautiful bride waiting for your groom. Jesus will come for you, then you'll dance the night away." His eyes stung and his throat tightened.

What looked like a small smile pulled at her thin lips. A peaceful expression passed across her face. "You have...diary...my life..."

"*Oui*. Julien gave it to me. Thank you, *Mamie*. It'll help me feel close to you."

Her eyes closed then. Julien stood on the other side of her bed. He touched her shoulder. "Rest now, Isabelle. We'll go in the kitchen for a while."

They turned to leave her bedside when the downstairs bell buzzed. "I'll see who it is." Julien walked to the door and pushed the interphone. He said something Luc didn't hear, then allowed the visitor to enter. "It's your father. His flight arrived today. He's coming from the airport."

Luc's eyes widened in surprise, but he was glad. His dad had barely enough time to see his mother before she was gone. Hopefully.

When the doorbell buzzed, Julien let Luc's father in. The man rushed into the room, his rumpled face a mask of worry. He greeted Julien and Luc with a nod before going to his mother's bedside.

Fabrice sat in a nearby chair and took her hand. She opened her eyes and stared at him a moment before smiling. "*T'es venu*...You...came." Her words were barely audible.

Julien and Luc went to the kitchen to give mother and son time together, however much she could still offer. Luc's stomach rumbled. "Can we get something to eat? I haven't had lunch."

They found fixings for a simple sandwich, fruit, and yogurt in the fridge. By the time they finished eating, Luc's father came into the kitchen.

"She's asleep now." Fabrice slumped into a chair across from them at the small kitchen table.

"Are you hungry, Dad?" His father nodded and Luc rose to make him a sandwich. "Did you have a chance to talk, or was she asleep?"

His dad's face softened, which Luc had almost never seen. "Yes. It wasn't much, but we were able to put our dispute behind us. Whatever it was." He stared out the window as tears filled his eyes. "So much wasted time...not speaking. Not being in contact..."

"I'm glad you talked before..." Luc swallowed, unable to say the words. He turned to the counter to finish making his father's sandwich then set the plate before him.

Julien stood. "I'll sit with her and let you know if there's any change. Help yourselves to anything else in the fridge."

Luc and his father sat alone at the table. Seconds of silence elapsed. Luc wondered what to say.

"Did you have a chance to talk to Freddie?" His dad's question didn't surprise him, despite the inappropriate circumstances, since they had little else they could talk about.

"Yeah, I emailed him before I came here and spoke with him once. I'm sure you know he offered me the job."

Despite his haggard appearance, Luc's father smiled. "Good, good. I put in a word for you."

"Thanks, but I didn't need it." It wasn't a time for irritation, but Luc couldn't stop the thread that snaked into his throat. "He had my resume. It stood on its own merit."

"Right, I know. But I've known Freddie a few years, and I didn't think it would hurt. Seems like it's right up your alley."

"Might be. I haven't decided."

His father blinked. "Well, what are you waiting for?"

Luc's eyes widened. "For one thing, *Mamie* is hanging by a thread in the next room." His voice rose. "Doesn't seem the right time. Freddie understands that."

"I know, but you've been here a few days already."

"*I'll* decide the right time, Dad."

"You always did do things your own way."

"As I *should*. Since I'm an adult. Since I'm not you."

Fabrice waved the air. "Ah, we're a lot alike, you know. But you always had that stubborn streak."

Something hot and prickly stirred in Luc's stomach. "Being an individual who makes his own choices isn't the same as being stubborn. I'm not stubborn if I don't follow exactly in your footprints. Having similar strengths and abilities doesn't make me your mini-me."

Fabrice chuckled. "There are worse things."

"No, there aren't, Dad. If you raise a son to be exactly like you, don't you know you've failed as a father?" Luc's words hung in the air as he stared at his dad. Tension crackled. It had to be said. It was time. "All my life, it was all about you. I never had any validation of my own gifts, my own accomplishments as a kid growing up because you made sure everyone was in your shadow." His voice had risen yet remained cold. "Especially me."

His father drew up his shoulders. A frown etched deep lines on his once handsome face. "You ungrateful—"

"Oh, was I supposed to be grateful to be shoved into your mold? That's not the role of a father. I figured out what you wanted at a young enough age to spare me from becoming you. Dad, I don't want to be you. I've never wanted to be you. You may be smart and successful, but your heart is hard and self-absorbed. Mom follows you like a planet in your solar system instead of being the deeply loved and cherished woman she deserves to be." Luc stood. He had to say his piece, to stop his father from retorting, or he'd never get the truth across. It might cost him, but he had to do it. Thirty years too late.

"While I was here, I saw Meghan. Do you remember her? She was here on vacation. A year and a half ago, we broke up because I chose a job over our relationship. In that, I resembled you perfectly, putting myself above someone I loved. I'm not doing that again. So, if she wants me to give up the job with Freddie, I'll do it."

"That would be a mistake. Your career—"

"Yes, my career was more important than love at one time, but it isn't anymore. I made that mistake, and it cost me Meghan." Suddenly something else was crystal clear to him, and he almost flinched at the realization.

"Women come and go, Luc," his father spluttered. "You're building something. You didn't make a mistake."

"Yes, I did. So, despite my so-called stubbornness to find my own way, I still ended up chasing what I thought would make *you* proud of me. Consciously, I wanted to do anything *but* what you were doing. Told myself I didn't care what you thought, since all you cared about was yourself." Huh. Despite his continual efforts. His voice dropped. "I guess every guy wants his dad to be proud of him. Even if it's subconscious. Even if he runs the opposite way, he'll end up trying anyway."

Julien peered around the kitchen door and gestured at them to keep the volume down.

Luc nodded at him and lowered his voice. "Dad, I'm done with that. Jobs don't define me. I'm not worth more because I make six figures, or because I keep getting promoted. Life is much more than that."

He stopped. Breathed deeply. He'd said enough. Now his dad would ream him out, disown him, whatever. It was fine. *He* was fine. Because nothing his dad said or did defined him. God defined him as a beloved son who had his own gifts, his own path designed uniquely for him.

But his dad didn't retort, didn't insult him. His jaw stiffened, and he stared at Luc with what seemed to be shock or possibly understanding. At a loss for words for the first time ever. "I...I'm sorry you felt that way, son." He shook his head, then dropped his gaze to the table. "I did that because I *was* proud of you. I thought I knew what was good for you."

Luc blinked in disbelief. "You mean yourself? I don't want to be like you. Why can't we enjoy what we have in common without me being in your shadow? Have you noticed, Dad, I'm thirty-one years old? An adult. At my age, you had kids. If Meghan takes me, I'll marry her. If I have to give up this job to do it, I will." If only he could get her to talk to him again, that would be a start.

Before his eyes, Luc's abrasive, obnoxious dad seemed to shrink in his chair. His shoulders drooped and his eyes lost their fire. Who *was* this guy? Where was the arrogance Luc had seen every day of his young life?

"I'm sorry for everything, Luc. Just for the record, I *am* proud of you."

Luc swallowed, hesitant to believe what he was hearing. Time to lay down the sword. "Thanks for saying that, Dad."

Julien entered the room. "Sounds quiet in here. That's good." Julien the peacemaker. Luc let out a chuckle in spite of the storm that had just occurred. In the place of his anger, a wave of gratitude stole over him. His father's response was the last thing he'd expected.

"How is she?" Luc asked. "Still sleeping?"

"Yes. She looks very peaceful, but might not make it more than a day." Julien turned to Luc's dad. "Fabrice, about the apartment..."

"She told me she wanted to give it to me." Fabrice's voice emerged dull, flinty. "I told her that's not why I came. She said she knows that."

"She probably didn't have a chance to tell you about the arrangement we made." Julien sat across from Fabrice and folded his weathered hands on the table. "We didn't know if you'd come before she left us, or if you were even able to come. She signed it over to me with the idea that we transfer it to you anytime afterward. And since you are here, before you leave, we'll meet with the *notaire* she works with."

Luc's father sighed, then leveled a stare at Julien. "Julien, you should have it. You've been by her side for what, thirty years? Twenty at least."

Julien's eyes widened. "No, Fabrice. It's for you. It's worth a lot of money."

But Luc's father frowned. "I don't need the money. You probably don't either, but it's right that you should have it. Give it to your grandchildren. Or rent it out for income. You deserve it."

"You're sure, Fabrice?"

"Yes, I'm sure." He met Luc's gaze. "It's a day to do the right thing."

Julien blinked, his expression hardly changing, though emotion showed in his eyes. "Then, thank you."

Silence, peaceful instead of tense, settled in the kitchen.

Just then, Brigitte rushed in. "I think…I think she's gone."

Chapter Fourteen

Meghan regretted having chosen a window seat on the massive airplane headed to Atlanta. For a daytime flight, she liked being able to access the aisle more easily. At least it was direct. She'd be home before dinnertime. Though home seemed like a foreign concept after two weeks in paradise.

She gazed listlessly at the baking tarmac as flight attendants made final preparations for take-off. Thankfully, the seat on her left remained empty, giving her a greater impression of being alone to think bittersweet thoughts. Her moments before Luc arrived were sweet, then sweeter after. Then bitter, all over again. Every time she opened her heart...

A smiling blond flight attendant passed along the rows, then several minutes later, they were airborne. Meghan released the tension in her shoulders and back, but couldn't do much for the empty cavern inside.

Luc had expected her to follow him, just like the last time. He hadn't actually said that, but she could tell. Once again, she'd be the one to sacrifice, and they weren't even engaged. He'd said they'd work it out, that it was just one option. Had she made a mistake by assuming they wouldn't make it as a couple? Again?

The question clawed inside her. She'd told Luc she'd regretted being stubborn, blocking his number, refusing to talk about it. Was she doing the same thing, despite the miraculous second chance they'd been given?

A painful lump settled in her throat. She'd done the same thing twice with the man she claimed to love. The question was, why?

"Is it okay if we lower the shade?" The voice of the twenty-something traveler two seats over broke into Meghan's thoughts.

"Sure, no problem." Meghan complied, sorry to lose the daylight and ever-changing cloud formations outside the window.

She'd been sure Luc hadn't changed. But maybe *she* was the one who hadn't changed. He'd said he didn't want to lose her again. He'd opened a dialogue with her, a brainstorm, even if it was clear he wanted the Illinois job. It was what she'd *wanted* him to do the first time.

But like the last time, she'd blown a fuse. Refused to listen. Had her tantrum. Had she wanted him to sacrifice for her, the way he'd expected *her* to do the last time? Was it simply revenge on her part? No, not that. But she didn't know what it was.

An image flashed in her mind. Her older sisters complaining about what a baby she was. How she wanted all the attention, when all she'd wanted was to be included. To be wanted. They were twins, six years older. As an adult, she understood why they wouldn't want her around, but at the time, it hurt. Her mother had waved it away, busy doing something else. Meghan had always wanted to be special, instead of an afterthought. The accidental pregnancy that made her like an only child. The mere chance occurrence, unplanned.

Some things hadn't changed. She still wanted to be special to someone. And often, was pushy and controlling enough to insist on it, just like a spoiled only child. An argument she'd had with Adam recently came to mind. Seemed petty now, but she'd held her ground, refusing to budge. He'd called her *high maintenance*, saying he had to walk on eggshells to keep her from blowing up.

Meghan winced. Was that true? It had been that day. And it wasn't long after that when Adam distanced himself from her little by little, until a breakup was inevitable.

Lord, am I high maintenance? Do I demand everyone else to treat me like I'm special, like I deserve something? She clenched her fists through her silent prayer, now grateful for the darkness in the cabin. *Or like someone with such a fragile self-*

esteem that everyone walks on eggshells? Her eyes stung as a heavy wave of truth flowed through her. *My self-esteem should be based on what you say about me, Lord, not what other people do or don't do.*

Tears rolled down her cheeks. She rummaged in the purse sitting near her feet and pulled out a tissue, then several. She'd need them. She had more to say, more to surrender. *Then there are the grudges. Lord. Multiple grudges spanning years. Father, who am I to hold a grudge after all you've done for me, sacrificing yourself for me? Who am I to demand special attention when you've given me everything? How can I have people on the hook for things? I'm tired of being angry. I thought it made me feel stronger, but it keeps me from feeling whole.*

Luc had been so patient. He might still be a workaholic, but had tried to do things differently this time. Why hadn't she seen it then, before it was too late? A mental movie of the previous evening rewound in her head...of herself in a huff as she put up her wall against him, as she demanded her way. Then that morning when she quietly left the apartment, knowing he'd arrive later to take her to the airport. How must he have felt, after trying so hard to reason with her? And the worst thing, she loved him and still turned him away for the second time. On what basis? Her pride and neediness? Her refusal to give up her *job*? She'd done the same thing he'd done when he went to Texas. And now, she wouldn't get another chance with Luc Badaux.

At that thought, a sob escaped her throat, and more tears trickled down her cheeks. Tears couldn't change the events, but they might change her future. That was not the woman she wanted to be, someone who made people tiptoe around her, afraid of her anger and grudges, treating her like she was special simply because they're afraid not to. She'd done that with boyfriends, craving their attention. After a while, they'd gotten tired and had broken off with her. Luc would have eventually done the same thing. Maybe that's exactly why he went to Texas without her.

Lord, that's not who I want to be. I don't want to lose people I love, including family relationships and friends because I hold them to too high of a standard. Either they walk away, or I do. Lord, that's not the way you taught me. That's not the example you set, either.

Her boss, Emily, floated into her mind. She didn't know whether Emily understood God's grace, but she'd offered grace and forgiveness to Meghan when she'd made a serious mistake at work. Meghan wanted to be like that. Full of grace, flowing with God's love for others, not looking out for her own needs, her own importance.

She prayed her confession for all the people she'd pushed away or driven away, including Luc, Adam, her sisters, her mother. And God. By creating a spiny layer of self-protection, she'd held him at arm's length. She'd deprived him of his desire to fight her battles, to be her hiding place.

By the time Meghan arrived in Atlanta, she'd had crossed the ocean and eaten a mediocre meal and a snack. But she'd also spent eight hours doing business with God. Though her eyes were puffy, and she felt wrung out, she also felt washed clean, determined to be different with God's help. She couldn't control Luc, Adam, her mother, or anyone else, and no longer wanted to. But step by step, she could align herself with who God wanted her to be. Full of grace, following his leading, instead of forcing her own way. Maybe that's why he took her to Nice in the first place. Maybe it wasn't about Luc Badaux at all.

ೞ ೞ ೞ

Despite Luc's love of Nice, he was ready to leave. It hadn't exactly been uneventful or relaxing. He sipped his first espresso of the day on the Riquier balcony while gazing at tile rooftops and wrought iron gracing each window in his view. A blanket of calm lay on the streets below, since it was Sunday morning.

Meghan would be back in Atlanta by now, not yet awake. And his beloved *Mamie* would be in heaven. The thought of both women caused sadness, heaviness inside him.

His phone rang. Julien.

"Good morning, Luc." Though Julien was a reserved man, his voice carried a solemn note. "I must give you the news that your grandmother passed away early this morning. Last night while we were there, she slipped into a coma, and she died around three o'clock this morning. I've told your father. We'll have a simple Mass for her on Wednesday morning."

"Thanks for letting me know, Julien." Luc spoke through a lump in his throat. "Are you doing okay?"

"Yes, I'm fine. I knew this was coming. I'll miss her, as you will. But I'm relieved for her too. I'm glad your father made it before she left us."

"I am too. I was surprised but glad. I'll probably stay until Friday. I'll be here to help with anything you need. Please don't hesitate."

When Luc disconnected, he texted his mom and Max. Then he went online to book his return flight and notify his boss that he'd be back in the office the following Monday. After his second cup of coffee and half a baguette, he slipped *Mamie*'s diary into a small shoulder bag and headed to the waterfront.

A few people strolled the wide concrete boardwalk or the pebbly beach, but it was an otherwise sleepy Sunday morning. Aside from a few people reading their phones or books, Luc had the benches to himself. He spent the first half hour watching the waves, allowing them to calm his emotions, which refused to be calmed. And he prayed. He prayed for renewal in his faith. For direction. For Meghan.

His thoughts returned frequently to *Mamie* as he mentally leafed through a cascade of memories of her. Laughing around the table with her and *Papi*, water balloon fights on her lawn with Max, conversations about God when he'd had troubling questions about life. Despite the band of pain gripping his heart, he smiled, remembering the grand reunions they'd had after moving to the States and returning to visit Nice each summer. "Thank you, *Mamie*, for a rich life full of memories. Memories of your love." His throat felt thick. Tears stung his eyes and squeezed out of the corners, where he let them fall. "Thank you for being a wonderful grandmother, and for the faith you gave me." His whispered words disappeared in the sound of the waves.

A faith he needed to strengthen. Yet, it had already begun. Seeing his father's response to his heartfelt but harsh words had humbled him. He'd thought his father too hardened to receive anything Luc had to say, yet last night, he'd heard the raw truth from Luc. It might open their relationship and allow them to be closer. Or at least get along more peacefully.

His mind returned to the sudden revelation he'd experienced while arguing with his father—that he'd moved to different jobs, sought bigger challenges, higher salaries, higher positions in part to prove his worth to his dad. And he'd never understood it had been the force driving him. All his life, he strove to be the anti-Fabrice, when all the while he'd been asking, begging for his approval. For validation. If anyone had told him this even three weeks ago, he'd have laughed in their faces.

For years he'd considered it natural to do those things, to seek bigger and better jobs. He'd seen his dad do it all his life, so he also had a role model. Luc made a sound in his throat. What a misguided life he'd led. He'd enjoyed his careers, but had missed so much along the way.

Like Meghan. How many times had he worked late when he didn't have to and ended up squeezing in time with her? He'd impressed the boss, but at what price? Even his dad hadn't noticed. Meghan hadn't complained at first, but her patience had worn thin. That could be what he'd witnessed two days ago, when she quietly backed away, refusing a repeat performance with a workaholic boyfriend.

If all that wasn't bad enough, Luc hadn't understood his true identity. Having a strong resume and good annual reviews, unsolicited job offers...none of that weighed anything in God's economy. God said he was a son with value just *because*. No need to prove himself to anyone, including himself. He needed to tap into that truth once again. It had been too long. *Lord, make me a better man. Set me free from the idols of work and career. That's what they are. You gave us work for our fulfillment and benefit, but we make it into an idol too often. I'm guilty of doing it.*

If only God would do another miracle with Meghan. Open her heart. Open a new door. Give them another chance. That's all he asked. *Lord, about Meghan—if it's your will...*

Maybe it wasn't.

A pair of seagulls shrieked overhead, then chased each other along the shoreline until they flew out of sight. He sighed. Even though he and Meghan were finished—again—he'd learned the lesson early enough to salvage the rest of his working years. He'd learn to pace himself and understand what was most important in his life. He'd measure his accomplishments according to his personal best while keeping balance in his own life, instead of running a mad race to accomplish more than anyone else.

Luc opened the flap of his canvas *sacoche* (Meghan called it his man purse), and pulled out the diary. He flipped through the first few pages and saw a variety of dates from *Mamie*'s life, with large gaps between. The accounts began when she and *Papi* moved to the Cote d'Azur area, when they had two young children, his father, Fabrice, and his younger brother, Damien, who'd died of cancer twenty years earlier. She wrote about how she missed some of her friends back in Grenoble, where she'd grown up. A few pages later, after a gap of a year or so, her tone had changed. Instead, she described how much she loved the climate and the sea. Luc tilted his head to look at a shady palm tree overhead. It wasn't at all difficult to adjust to this.

The next gap spanned at least twenty years. The book in his hands must cover his grandmother's entire adult life. No wonder she wanted to read through it before her life ended. In it, she wrote about *Papi*, about her sons as they grew into adults. The diary touched on the broad lines of everything she'd experienced over the previous fifty years.

A review of her adult life before it ended.

Her rounded handwriting warmed him with its familiarity. And the honesty of some of her observations about people or situations stirred him to chuckle more than once. Though he wouldn't see her again this side of heaven, he felt she'd invited him to glimpse a deeper level of her life and thoughts.

He skimmed the next few pages, noting the dates until he got to the most recent, around twelve years ago. Around the time *Papi* died.

We buried Claude last month. My Claude. He promised me we'd grow old together, but here I am by myself. When he had that first stroke, he said he'd slow down, but he didn't. In his mind, providing was everything, and he provided well. He needed to, I guess. He told me it would give us a comfortable retirement and we could do what we wanted to. And we did for two years. Two short years. Claude, they were too short.

The handwriting became messier, as if *Mamie*'s distress emerged through her pen. *Why didn't you work less and live longer so we could be together, like you promised? I wouldn't have cared to have less money and fewer houses. You said we'd have all our time together and the means to enjoy whatever we wanted. Instead, I have a nice apartment in a chic neighborhood, but I don't have you. I think you know what I'd prefer.*

The entry ended with only a few blank pages remaining. Luc sat still, feeling a weight inside. His *Papi* had been a good provider, to the point of leaving behind three apartments on the Cote d'Azur. No small accomplishment, plus other holdings he had elsewhere. But what did it all mean if he died as soon as he stopped working? He left behind two sons who were like strangers to him and the woman he'd loved all those years. They'd waited for him to retire so they could be together. Except they were *already* together. As she'd said, she'd have preferred simply being with him. A simpler lifestyle, perhaps, and more of him. *Papi* had sacrificed for his family, but *Mamie* had sacrificed far more.

Luc wouldn't make that mistake. He'd been headed down the same road as both his grandfather and his father. He'd break the chain, and teach his sons to do the same, once he had some. Hopefully, with Meghan.

Meghan, who he loved more than he wanted to prove himself.

He let those thoughts settle as the pieces moved around inside him. The message was clear, like a bullhorn. *I'm hearing you, Lord. You're resetting the balance for my whole life.* The weight evaporated, like a humid cloud floating away in the breeze. A feeling of hope glided through him. He had choices. From now on, he'd make the right ones.

Luc glanced at the time on his phone. He stood and stretched his legs. His butt ached from sitting on the bench for over an hour, but he also had an appointment with Sébastien. Since he was in France, they'd discuss some business related to the rental properties. Nothing they couldn't do over the phone. But since it *was* France, they could only discuss business at a restaurant with a bottle of Provence rosé.

Chapter Fifteen

"Hey, Dad. It's Meghan." The tiny patio behind her garden-level apartment baked under June sunshine. Soon, it would be too hot to enjoy.

"You're back from France. How's my girl?"

Meghan loved the sound of her father's voice, as long as he wasn't sick or angry. It wove a net of comfort and connection around her heart. "You sound fully recovered and normal. Are you?" She pulled her sunglasses from the top of her head and settled them on her nose.

"Pretty much. Jill takes good care of me."

Meghan laughed. "Is she there in the room and you're getting brownie points?"

"No, it's true. And she's smiling and says hi. When did you get back?"

"Last night."

"You must still be tired, then. We'd love to hear about your trip once you're rested."

"Yeah, of course. I owe you a visit. Hey, guess who I ran into in Nice." The casual tone of her voice belied the pinch inside as she said the words.

"Can't guess. Gerard Départdieu? Juliette Binoche?"

She chuckled. "Well, one of them might own a villa on a cliffside, but no. I saw Luc Badaux. Remember him?"

For a moment, her dad fell silent. "How could I forget, Meggie? He broke your heart. You just ran into him there by chance?"

No, not by chance. More by divine intervention. Meghan told her dad the details of seeing Luc and how they'd briefly gotten back together before they broke up again.

"Oh, I'm sorry to hear that. Are you okay?"

"Uh, sure..." Sudden tears sprang into her eyes. "No, that's not quite true. I love him, Dad. He just got this job offer in Illinois, and I was so afraid he'd do the same thing as before, then I...I shut him out. Just like last time. *I* was the one who turned away both times." By the time she finished her phrase, tears coursed down her cheeks.

"Is it too late?" Her dad's voice was gentle. "Sounds like you regret that and want it to work." Her father had always liked Luc, but tried to stay neutral in her relationships.

"I'm not sure how to undo what I did. Or how to reach him in Texas." And yet...a sudden spark of hope flickered inside her. "But we *did* exchange phone numbers, I just remembered." And there were three messages from him she'd never responded to.

In her hurt, she'd ignored them. Back when hurt was a way of life. Which it no longer was.

"I'll call him, once I'm sure he's back from France. I don't know how long he'll be there, because of his grandmother." He might write Meghan off well before then.

"Might be worth a try, since you love him."

She sniffed and nodded, rubbing moisture from her eyes. She *did* love him. And she would *not* give up so easily anymore. Beyond that decision, she didn't have a strategy. "Dad, I thought a lot about the grudge. Grudges. Like we talked about before I left for France. And I thought about it even more after my fight with Luc. I don't want to be that person anymore. I want to have a long fuse and a short memory of differences."

"You have so many nice qualities, Meggie," her father said. "Anger isn't one of them." He followed with a chuckle, which lightened the harsh truth.

A sharp twinge pinched inside. "I know. I...I've given up on it. Officially."

"I'm glad to hear it. Keep me posted on things with Luc, if you want to. Now that I'm on the mend, we'd love to see you. Come for a visit. We're not that far away."

"I will, Dad. Well, just wanted to check on you and let you know I'm back. Say hi to Jill for me."

She had more phone calls to make, starting with Shane. That would be an easy call, since she had no barriers with her best friend. When there was no answer, Meghan realized she must be at church. "Hi Shane, it's Meghan. I just got home last night. Give me a call when you have time today. I have lots of news about my trip." Shane knew the background about Luc, though not the current episode. She tended to side with Meghan, knowing only her account. Once Meghan admitted her immature response, Shane might confront her, which she'd deserve.

Next up, the harder calls, starting with her sisters. "Hi Jenn." Meghan hadn't spoken to her sisters, Jenn and Mia, for many months. Maybe last Christmas. But Jenn wasn't available either. "It's Meghan. I know we haven't talked in a while, and I want that to change. I'm sorry I haven't kept in better touch." It went both ways, but she'd take the first step. "Give me a call when you have time. I'd love to catch up."

She left a similar message for her sister, Mia. Now, for her mother. A memory arose in her mind. One day, her sisters had gone to the mall and left Meghan behind. She'd gone crying to her mother, who'd bent down and enclosed her in an embrace. "Know what we'll do together?" She'd given seven-year-old Meghan a conspiratorial smile. "We'll make cookies. Want to?" And they had, giggling together, as mouth-watering aromas filled the kitchen. *So much better than going to the mall.*

At the memory, a wave of tenderness flooded Meghan's chest. Her dear mother, who she'd shunned for years.

She took her phone and tapped her mother's number. A wave of relief surged at the sound of her voice. "Hi, Mom, it's me, Meghan."

"Meghan, what a nice surprise."

"I was thinking about how seldom I call you, and I want to change that, Mom. I'm so sorry. My phone calls should never be a surprise. I want to keep in touch better with you."

"I would love that, sweetie."

Meghan thought she heard her mother's voice thicken with emotion.

"Mom, I want to apologize to you for my attitude since you and Dad split up." Her voice came out in a rush. She had to say it before she lost her nerve. "I know that's been years now, but I acted like a judgmental, spoiled brat. I'm glad you're happy with Bert. At the time, I judged you for your decision and allowed a wall to develop. I'm sorry, Mom."

"Thank you, Meghan. I was sorry we weren't as close anymore. I...I didn't think there was anything I could do. Do you think you can come soon for a visit?"

"I'd love to. I'll come up for a long weekend later this summer or early fall. I'd like to get to know Bert better too, after all these years. And in the meantime, I'll call more often. I promise." So many years wasted.

She'd meant it. She'd act on her decisions to be different. If only she'd had this change of heart in time to salvage her reunion with Luc.

Luc. She wanted to make up for her childish response in Nice, but how? She took her phone in her hand, still warm from her previous calls. *What should I say, Lord? What do you want my response to be?*

She should tell Luc what she should have told him in Nice. He should take the job in Illinois, and they'd pursue their relationship long-distance until they knew what the next step was. By faith, peacefully and patiently.

Why had she been resistant to that idea? She'd been afraid to lose him again and wanted closure so badly, she ended up making *sure* she lost him. Again. She shook her head at her own stupidity.

Before she lost her nerve she texted him her apology, then backspaced. She tried again, and it didn't sound right. Finally, she typed, *I love you, Luc. I'm sorry. Take the job and we'll keep in touch.*

ಌ ಌ ಌ

The visitors who'd gathered at the Catholic church in Beaulieu were more numerous than Luc had expected, given the few days Julien had to notify them of Isabelle's passing. Chandeliers overhead bathed the stone walls with warmth and muted light. The priest's words echoed in the cavernous space. "Let us consider this verse from First Thessalonians, which applies today," he said. "'And now, dear brothers and sisters, we want you to know what will happen to the believers who have died so you will not grieve like people who have no hope.'"

Luc shot a glance at his father who, as far as he knew, was a typical French skeptic. How did those words affect him? Did they touch his doubting stance even slightly? Or were they simply words that skimmed across his ears without his even hearing them? The rigid mask on his expressionless face told nothing of what was happening inside. Was he thinking about his next work project at home, or regretting the last few years that he and his mother hadn't spoken?

Scanning the small crowd, Luc wondered the same thing about them. *Mamie* had invested in people all her life. The friends in her neighborhood, at her church. The people whose businesses she frequented regularly. They were all here remembering, acknowledging the impact she'd made. What or who had *he* invested in? Work. A friend or two, though mostly superficially. Max was his friend as well as his brother. Did he need others?

Yes, in fact, he did. He hadn't realized it before, since he'd always worked too hard.

His mind went to Meghan, as it frequently did. She'd sent a cryptic text a few days ago. Though he was glad she'd reached out, he hadn't known what she meant or how to respond, so he hadn't yet.

After the service, clusters of *Mamie*'s friends gathered, talking in low tones among themselves. Some recognized Fabrice and Luc, offering condolences and kind words about *Mamie*.

"It was a nice service," offered Julien. There seemed to be little else to say.

And yet, there was plenty to say. "It was," Luc said. "What strikes me is the hope she had, even as she was dying. For most people, their only hope and purpose is what they can accomplish, buy, and be known for. But it's like a drop of rain in the ocean. It's gone, and no one remembers or cares."

Fabrice shot Luc an annoyed, or perhaps uncomfortable glance as they left the church. But Luc wasn't finished. "We spend most of our adult lives investing in something no one cares about, then we die. Even a year later, everyone has moved on to other things. *Papi* spent his life working hard, then died as soon as he retired. At least *Mamie* understood what was important."

"Is that your new philosophy?" Luc's father smirked. "You're going to go live at the ski slopes and the beach now?"

Luc stared at his father, emboldened by his new understanding. "You don't get it, do you, Dad? No, I'm not going to do that. Nothing's wrong with good, honest work, but if that's all we have...we miss out on the important people around us. Not to mention eternity afterward, which is a whole lot longer." He shook his head. "I hope *you'll* learn something before you follow in *Papi's* footsteps."

His father grunted a response. They fell silent and returned to Julien's car. Fortunately, there was no burial, since *Mamie* had wanted to be cremated. She'd arranged everything in detail before becoming weak and bedridden.

And now, she was dancing in eternity.

ଔ ଔ ଔ

Saturday morning, Meghan finished her coffee and breakfast at the eat-in bar of her kitchen. The day stretched out before her, already scheduled with tasks on her to-do list. Last weekend was for reflection and restoration of relationships. *This* weekend was for catching up on housework, bills, and any other neglected matters following her trip and her return to work.

She'd gone into the office Monday morning, feigning joy and refreshment after her trip. Her colleagues asked how her vacation was and wanted to see photos. Meghan showed a few photos on her phone, but skipped those of Luc. She hadn't deleted them, and wouldn't.

Emily had welcomed her with a warm smile, convinced Meghan's involuntary time off had renewed and energized her. The workload waiting for her was an indication of that.

After putting in full days at work for the entire week, France felt light years away, lost amidst her new batch of responsibilities. Luc seemed even farther, though memories of their moments together—visiting golden places, being in his arms, feeling they were given a second chance—weren't far from her mind, despite her efforts to concentrate on the present. He hadn't called, likely sure he'd be stonewalled again, nor had he responded to her text. That spoke painful volumes. Finally, she'd been willing to put him before everything else, to follow him to Illinois if he wanted her to. But he'd apparently had enough. The realization burned a hole in her stomach. But what else could she expect?

Postcard from Nice Kyle Hunter

Two strikes, he was out. Or maybe he'd finally decided to push her out of *his* life, preferring a new chapter in Illinois, diving into the challenge of a new job. Finding a new girlfriend with whom he didn't have to walk on eggshells.

A third iteration for Luc and Meghan likely wouldn't come. Once she knew he was back in the States, she'd chance a phone call, even if he didn't respond to her text. Then and only then, she'd give up.

Meghan rose and straightened the kitchen. Time to tackle her list, but her energy bottomed out when she thought about it. She could start with the stack of nonessential mail on the coffee table. That would be an easy way to begin. She slumped onto the couch and pulled the stack onto her lap, unwilling to look at the first envelope.

The doorbell rang. Unusual. Likely, someone selling something. She'd look through the peephole and ignore it. Meghan tiptoed to the door and looked out, seeing no one. But something sat on the front porch. She eased the door open and looked down at a stunning pastel bouquet of lilies, carnations, and sweet peas. Her heart thumped as she took it inside. A tiny card dangled from one of the stems. She set the arrangement on the coffee table and fumbled with the card.

My Meghan, you are always in my heart and my thoughts. Please don't give up on us. We can work things out. I love you. Luc.

She gasped. One hand raised to her mouth. "Luc!" Oh, Luc. He'd sent her flowers from France. Or Texas. There was hope for them. *Thank you, Lord!* Luc hadn't given up on her. He still loved her.

The doorbell sounded again. She returned to the door and squealed when she saw a familiar lanky stance through the peephole. She pulled the door open. "Luc!"

He stood there on her porch, handsome as ever, with his lopsided grin. "Come in!" She stood aside to let him enter, then went into his arms. They circled around her, and the two of them held onto each other like a tangle of string. After several minutes, she pulled her head back and her eyes searched his face. "You came—"

He cut off her words with his lips. The next few seconds took Meghan back to paradise...not Nice or the French Riviera. Luc's arms around her, his lips on hers, his love pouring into and through her.

She caught her breath after his kiss. "You didn't answer my text, so I thought it...it was over."

"Over?" His brows furrowed, though he didn't let go of her. "I thought *you* were saying it was over, but you wanted to stay friends. I didn't know what you meant."

Meghan laughed and buried her head in his chest. "I must be as bad a communicator as you used to be."

"Me? I think I've improved a lot."

They grinned at each other. "Yes, you really have," she said. "Maybe you can teach *me*."

"We can start right now..." He leaned forward and kissed her again for several wonderful moments.

"How did you find where I live?" she asked as they pulled apart. She led him to the couch, afraid to let go of his hand.

He shot her a smug smile as he sat beside her. "You rented an apartment from me, remember? Sébastian had everything I needed."

"Of course, he did." Laughter bubbled up inside like uncorked champagne. "Thank you for the gorgeous flowers." She touched some of the silken petals on the coffee table and added a coy smile. "Why didn't you bring them in yourself?" Though it had been clever of him to ring twice and heighten the suspense.

"So many questions." He scooted closer to her. "After our last discussion, I thought it was wise to send a peace offering first." He winked. "Flowers then Luc."

"Not necessary, since I was mourning the way things ended in Nice. I'm sorry for my part. Which was everything." Her voice softened, and she touched his face, rough with a few neglected whiskers. "I need to tell you something."

"And I need to tell *you* something. I have two gifts for you."

"Let me tell you first. Please."

He waited, a smile curving his wonderful lips.

She placed her hands on his chest. "Luc, I'm sorry. I'm sorry I've always been kind of high maintenance, full of anger and grudges. I'm sorry I didn't listen to you and work things out in Nice. I was on the plane leaving for Nice and was thinking *you haven't changed, it won't work out*. As if it were again your fault and I was completely innocent. I pointed a finger at you, then as they say, my finger ended up pointing back at *me*. I realized how difficult I can be. I hope you'll forgive me."

"Oh, Meghan." He pulled her close and kissed her. "I love you, Meghan. I can't remember what I should forgive you for... Oh yeah, the grudges. Well, I'm glad you're done with those. I thought I'd just have to deal with it, since I need you in my life." He grinned, and she swatted him playfully.

His smile dimmed. "I hope you forgive me too. For being a workaholic in our past relationship. For not giving you the priority you always deserved. For not treating you as the precious woman I was blessed to be able to date. I learned about all that after you left, but I'll tell you about it later."

"I do forgive you, Luc. For everything. I'd already decided I'd forgive you even if we never got back together. Even if you married the six-foot Texan supermodel."

"Huh?" He gave her a quizzical look. "Now, why would I want that when I have a short, beautiful, sexy—" He kissed her lightly, then pulled back. "My turn. I have two gifts for you."

"So you said. A lavender sachet and Nice T-shirt, by any chance?"

He grinned. "Nope, better than that." He opened the man purse he often carried and pulled out two folded pieces of paper. "Read this one first." He handed one to her. "Then the other one." He tapped the second paper.

Now she was curious. She unfolded the first page and skimmed it. Her gaze met his. "It's a resignation. For the Texas job."

"Yes, it is. Now read the other one."

She did, and her eyes widened. "And this one turns down the Illinois job. I'm confused. You'd give up both of them?"

"If that's what you want. I said these were gifts for you because you can choose one or both of them. You can decide what the next step for us will be."

"Oh, Luc. I couldn't do that. You said we should decide together."

"I did. We tried that, and it wasn't the right time. Since I'm determined to stay with you and never leave, regardless of where we live, you can decide."

"Music to my ears." She couldn't suppress a smile. "Not me deciding, but you never leaving."

"I'll give you time to think about it, and we can still talk it over if you want to. But now for my third surprise. Or rather, a question. It's important, so listen carefully." He held up one finger, making sure he had her attention.

She looked at him with an expectant grin. "I'm listening."

Luc took both her hands in his. When his gaze locked hers, she saw mischief there. "If we were to get married, how much time would you want?"

Her mouth dropped open. She was about to speak when he placed his finger on her lips.

"I mean, if you want a big white wedding, that's fine, but it'll take a few months to plan. Now, if you don't mind about that as much, we can do it sooner. Like in a couple of weeks."

"Oh, Luc! I think that's a proposal, right?"

He laughed. "Yes, it is...*à ma façon.*" In his own way. "I want to marry you as soon as possible, if you'll have me."

"*Mais, oui!* Absolutely!"

"Sorry I'm not on my knees. This is more my style..." He leaned into her and pressed her back to the couch cushions then kissed her with such fervor, she felt like a pool of melted chocolate. Without shifting his position, he pulled his head back. "What do you think?" he whispered, as his eyes twinkled.

"Like I was able to think during *that* kiss?" She smiled at him. "I don't think I had any functioning brain cells just then."

Luc grinned. "You might need time to decide. Our future is in your hands."

"No, it's not, Bad Boy. We're together in *everything* from now on. But—"

"Yes?"

She struggled to a seated position. "I think a month would be about perfect. For the wedding, that is. That'll give me time to arrange a small ceremony with family and friends. Doesn't have to be huge. I arrange events all the time at work. This is doable." She already had a few ideas for small venues. The chapel at the church she attended, or a nice restaurant, depending on what was available. It *was* high wedding season, but God had already moved other obstacles.

"A month," he said. "I guess I can wait. I'll go ahead and resign from my current job."

"Are you sure?"

"Yes, absolutely. They won't let me work remotely. I've already asked."

"Maybe the other job will."

"Maybe they will." He stared at her with his hypnotic hazel-green eyes, then they roved her face, her lips. "That's not my first concern." His voice had dropped. "My primary concern is making you Mrs. Meghan Badaux as soon as possible."

"I like the sound of *that*."

Epilogue

One year later

The view from the fourth story never ceased to thrill Meghan, though they'd already been in Villefranche-sur-Mer for five months. Through the kitchen window, a sliver of turquoise blue from the Mediterranean competed with the flawless blue sky. If she shifted her gaze left, she saw terracotta roofs on yellow and orange buildings and palm trees stretching out to the horizon.

She gave the scrambled eggs a final stir and turned off the stove, then scooped them into a bowl. "Breakfast is ready," she called from the small kitchen to the back hall of the apartment where Luc was finishing his shower. "Can you come yet? We'll eat on the balcony."

Luc emerged from the hall, his hair spiky with water. He came to where she stood at the counter. With a gleam in his eye, he pulled her close and covered her neck with kisses. When his lips moved up to hers, she murmured with a giggle, "Eggs are getting cold."

He pulled back and grinned. "*Et alors?*" So? "How can I help?"

"*My* coffee is ready, but I know you like your espresso just so..."

"I had some already." He grabbed a bottle of orange juice and a basket of baguette pieces in one hand, and a container of butter in the other. "I'll take these. Meet you on the balcony. Then, over breakfast, we can decide what we're going to do for our first anniversary next month."

She lifted her brows in anticipation. "I'm happy I married a travel organizer. You know all the best places."

"*Mais, bien sûr.*" Of course. In the few months they'd lived in France, they'd traveled to Paris, Florence, Avignon and many of the little Provence towns around there...she lost track of what else. And of course, Nice. Where it had all begun...again.

They settled on the balcony. A June breeze floated off the nearby water, bathing them in a balmy embrace. "My favorite part of living in France." Meghan closed her eyes and breathed deeply of the morning air. "Breakfast on the balcony in warm months." She reached for Luc's hand and he prayed for the meal. She sipped her coffee...another pleasure, since everything tasted better in France. "Did you finish your current project for Freddie last night?"

"*Oui*. Done. I sent it at eleven last night, but he got it at five US time. Told him I'd have it to him by the time he left the office." The six-hour time difference was often an advantage for turning in projects on time. After moving into the two-bedroom apartment in Villefranche, Luc had set up an office for the two of them in one of the bedrooms. He worked full time remotely, and Meghan worked part time for an online event company.

Soon after their engagement the previous year, he'd resigned from the Texas job and accepted the job with Freddie on the condition that he be able to work remotely. Freddie was so impressed with Luc's resume and skills that he agreed to his conditions, as long as he could come to the office a couple of times a year and spend his first full month there getting oriented. They'd make their first trip back the following month. Meghan planned to travel with him so she could see her parents.

During Luc's first month in Chicago at the company, Meghan put all her organizational skills to work to plan their small wedding. Her sisters and their families had come to the small but elegant ceremony at her church, along with her parents, friends, colleagues, and Luc's family and friends. Then Luc moved to Atlanta.

A few months later, the subject of living in France for a year or more came up. It quickly became their obsession, as they researched what it would involve. Meghan had even been willing to quit her job in Atlanta and find something remote she could do in France, though Luc told her that financially, she didn't need to work full time or at all. Emily was the one who tipped Meghan off about an online event company looking for an experienced and organized employee.

Luc reached for the basket of sliced baguette. Meghan slid the butter dish to him. "Instead of Bad Boy, I need to start calling you Baguette Boy." They laughed.

"That's appropriate." Luc pulled three slices from the basket. "For our anniversary, I thought we might go to the Italian Lakes district. Does that appeal to you? I'll send you some links. You'll get excited when you see the photos."

Meghan smiled. "I trust your travel wisdom. How many days can you get off?"

He shrugged. "As many as I want, I guess. It's a special occasion. We can go for a week, okay?"

"Sounds great."

He finished spreading his baguette slice with butter, then laid down the knife. His hazel-green eyes met hers. They seemed to smoke with intensity as he took her hand. "This has been the happiest year of my life, Meghan. I want to celebrate that with you in a special way." He drew her hand to his lips and kissed it.

Meghan leaned toward him. "I feel the same." She'd never felt more complete, balanced, loved. It had been quite the year, changing everything about their lives, romantically, professionally, and geographically. Bringing them together—again—but also teaching both of them what it took to be happy together.

"You once told me you didn't have a romantic bone in your body," she said softly. "I just don't believe it anymore."

"After meeting you, I learned fast." He smirked. "Dumbest thing I ever did was move to Texas."

"I agree." She grinned. "But God has a way of doing what he wants, despite our big mistakes. Including mine. I was dumb too, because after you, no one else would cut it for me either."

"Sounds like we both got a lot smarter in the last couple years."

He leaned across the table and kissed her. It was a seal on the next year to come, and each year thereafter, erasing any gaps and promising so much more.

I hope you enjoyed reading, **Postcard from Nice**. If you did, please consider leaving a review for me. It would help other readers discover my books and be encouraged by their inspiring truths.

Do you enjoy stories that take place in Europe? Check out the following titles:

- Prodigals in Provence (Book 1 Love in Provence Series)
- A Promise in Provence (Book 2 Love in Provence Series)
- One December (Stand Alone Romance in Paris)
- Julia Redesigned (Second Chance Book 2, Florence, Italy)

Read Chapter One of all books (and/or purchase at numerous storefronts or eBooks direct from the author) at
www.Kyle-Hunter.com

Get a free novella, *Marissa Rewritten* (Book One in the *Second Chance Series*), when you sign up to receive my newsletter and updates about new books (and other insider goodies) at www.Kyle-Hunter.com.

More books...

Brenner Falls Romance Series

Come to the small town of Brenner Falls, Pennsylvania, where you'll make new friends and watch love blossom.

Good Gifts (Book One)

Nathan Chisholm's high-pressure job in the big city is interrupted by an inheritance he doesn't want, a struggling dinner theater. He returns to his hometown of Brenner Falls, Pennsylvania, so he can sell it fast and return to his normal life.

Leah Albright's plans for her life went up in smoke and she's forgotten how to dream. Instead, she spends her days at a dull job in Brenner Falls and her evenings with musical instruments and her cat. As holidays approach, she fakes cheer to stave off her disappointments.

Nathan and Leah rekindle the friendship they had in high school and attraction brews. But Nathan's leaving town once he sells the theater. And the residents of Brenner Falls, including Leah, don't want their beloved historic theater sold. And certainly not to the developer who's been lurking around.

Nathan finds himself trapped by well-meaning decisions and growing feelings for Leah. He may have gone too far to turn back from the risks to his future and his heart.

Custom Made (Book Two)

Blair McCartney's goal of becoming a fashion designer took a detour after an unplanned pregnancy. Eight years later, she's raising her son, Jake, in Brenner Falls and working in a clothing factory. Though she adores Jake, it's a far cry from the life she dreamed of.

Cooper Dawson, a contractor, still grieves the loss of his brother. He wraps up a housing project, then returns to Brenner Falls with his dog, Zipper. There, he wants to build his *own* dream house. In the meantime, he moves in next door to Blair and Jake.

What begins as a friendship blossoms into something deeper. Blair's rundown rental house presents its own challenges. Then, the sudden reappearance of Jake's biological father throws their lives—and budding romance—into turmoil, triggering old hurts, and testing the limits of faith and love.

Embracing the Broken (Book 3)

Physical therapist Amber Dawson strives to make life better for others. She'd love to leave the corporate atmosphere of her current job. If only she could buy the charming, abandoned house on the edge of town and open her own practice.

Ben Russo overcame a troubled youth and works as an engineer for the town of Brenner Falls. He's convinced the dilapidated house is historic and wants to prove it. Not only does he love history, but the discovery might also help him climb in his career.

When Amber and Ben meet at a wedding reception, the negative impression is mutual. But they later discover the little house they both have their eyes on is condemned unless they can prove it's historically significant. If the house is demolished, neither one will get it, so they decide to work together.

As Ben and Amber delve into the house's past, they encounter intrigue they never expected, and an attraction to each other they can't deny. But as they hit roadblocks to saving the broken-down house, they also come face to face with their own hidden brokenness and the grace that heals it.

More romantic stories by Kyle Hunter...

Romance in Provence Series

The Provence Series takes you with Bree and Lauren, best friends and business partners, to one of the loveliest regions of France. It's not always idyllic in the land of lavender fields and cliffside villages. Join Bree and Lauren as each woman discovers her unique journey... and surprising romance.

***Prodigals in Provence* (Book 1)**
Bree's Story

Bree Sorensen is living her dream as co-owner of a travel company that specializes in tours to Provence, France. But the latest trip isn't fully booked, adding financial strain to her already fragile business. In the land of idyllic lavender fields and cliffside villages, Bree wonders if she'll ever find peace from her troubled childhood, let alone save her career.

Travis Jeffries hides his emotional scars under the glitz of TV travel documentaries. A beloved public figure who often sniffs out travel scams, his smiling persona barely covers the pain of his failed marriage and missionary career years earlier. With his spiritual life a wasteland, Travis fears it's too late for God to welcome him back.

Travis seems like Bree's worst nightmare when she finds he has registered for her latest tour of Provence. One false move and her business could be ruined by his critique. But when attraction blossoms, will these two wounded believers find common ground?

A Promise in Provence (Book 2)
Lauren's Story

Lauren Abbott is at a turning point. She's just not sure *where* to turn. Her long-term relationship with Mark is fading fast. Instead, she feels drawn to Jean-Pierre, an attractive Frenchman she'd met the previous summer. When she's laid off from her job as a chef, she plans to go see him in Provence, France.

Mark can't get Lauren out of his heart, even though it's been close to a year since she asked him for space. When she goes to France, he's afraid he'll lose her for good. That is, until he goes there too, as a last-ditch effort to win her back.

At first, Lauren's angry that Mark has followed her to France. But a joint desire to help a young refugee boy leads them to work together. Lauren finds herself torn between Mark and Jean-Pierre. Worse, she's confronted with obstacles in helping the boy and even greater obstacles within herself.

Prodigals in Provence and A Promise in Provence are also available as a Boxset, *Love in Provence*. Both books in one volume.

The Second Chance Series

In *The Second Chance Series*, you'll meet Marissa, Julia, Sydney, and Eden, four college friends who, twenty-five years later, renew their friendships as they find themselves empty nesters and single again. You'll love getting to know these women and following each one in her own book. (Women's Fiction.)

Marissa Rewritten (Book 1: a Novella) An author becomes unblocked.

Julia Redesigned (Book 2) Discovery in Florence, Italy.

Sydney Rewound (Book 3) Present Clashes with the Past.

Eden Redefined (Book 4) Returning to College in Midlife.

Stand Alone Novels

One December (A Romance in Paris)

Circle Back Around (A Return Home to Save the Family Business)

Postcard from Nice *(A Novella set in Nice, France)*

About the Author

Kyle Hunter is the author of twelve novels of inspirational romance and women's fiction, weaving Christian truth into the lives of fictional people. Her relatable characters will become like close friends you'll cheer for and learn from as you join them on their journeys. Story settings range from Europe to small town America. As characters face outward and inward challenges, the spiritual and personal insights they gain are encouraging and relevant.

Kyle spent thirteen years living in France, and she's intrigued by faraway places. Currently, she lives in North Carolina where she writes fiction, non-fiction (under the pen name K. B. Oliver), and the travel blog OliversFrance.com. She also teaches French to adults.

Author's note

This year, I had the chance to spend a week in Nice. I'd been there previously, but never long enough to soak in the spirit of the city itself. This time, I fell in love with it! Like Meghan, I visited many of the surrounding towns as well. I'd go back in a heartbeat. (I'd even consider living for a while in Nice or Villefranche-sur-Mer!)

Before traveling, the idea of writing a stand-alone romance novella set in Nice grabbed me. I knew it was a romantic and gorgeous setting, perfect for a novel. That is the origin of this story!

You likely know that I am a Francophile, deeply interested in all things French. I've mentioned my travel blog, Oliver's France (Oliversfrance.com), which covers many wonderful destinations all over the country. (I am also K. B. Oliver.) If you're interested in seeing some towns you read about in *Postcard from Nice*, visit Oliver's France and do a search on Nice, Eze, and Antibes. I have two posts on Nice, one with day trips like the ones Meghan did.

If you're interested in travel French, check out my online course, Real French for Travelers (RealFrenchforTravelers.com) and/or find the free mini course on polite words and expressions at Oliver's France.

I hope this will inspire your future travels!

Postcard from Nice   *Kyle Hunter*

Postcard from Nice   *Kyle Hunter*

www.ingramcontent.com/pod-product-compliance
Lightning Source LLC
LaVergne TN
LVHW041914070526
838199LV00051BA/2613